THE BOAT ROCKER

THE BOAT ROCKER

HA JIN

PANTHEON BOOKS, NEW YORK

Copyright © 2016 by Ha Jin

All rights reserved. Published in the United States by Pantheon Books, a division of Penguin Random House LLC, New York, and distributed in Canada by Random House of Canada, a division of Penguin Random House Canada Limited, Toronto.

Pantheon Books and colophon are registered trademarks of Penguin Random House LLC.

Library of Congress Cataloging-in-Publication Data
Name: Jin, Ha, [date] author.
Title: The boat rocker : a novel / Ha Jin.
Description: First Edition. New York :
Pantheon Books [2016].
Identifiers: LCCN 2016007449 (print).
LCCN 2016016638 (ebook). ISBN 9780307911629
(hardcover). ISBN 9780307911636 (ebook).
Subjects: LCSH: Journalists—Fiction.
Investigative reporting—Fiction. Chinese—United
States—Fiction. BISAC: FICTION / Literary.
FICTION / Political.
Classification: LCC PS3560.16 B63 2016 (print).
LCC PS3560.16 (ebook). DDC 813/.54—dc23.
LC record available at: lccn.loc.gov/2016007449

www.pantheonbooks.com

Jacket design by Kelly Blair

Printed in the United States of America
First Edition
2 4 6 8 9 7 5 3 1

ALSO BY HA JIN

Between Silences

Facing Shadows

Ocean of Words

Under the Red Flag

In the Pond

Waiting

The Bridegroom

Wreckage

The Crazed

War Trash

A Free Life

The Writer as Migrant

A Good Fall

Nanjing Requiem

A Map of Betrayal

FOR CAO CHANGQING

THE BOAT ROCKER

ONE

A week before the fourth anniversary of 9/11, my boss, Kaiming, barged into my office, rattling a three-page printout in his hands. "Look at this, Danlin," he said, dropping the papers on my desk. "This is outrageous! How could they claim that George W. Bush had agreed to endorse a book by Yan Haili? Everyone can tell it's a lie the size of heaven."

I picked up the printout, an article from *The Yangtze Morning Post.* It raved about "a landmark novel," not yet released. I had recently signed a book contract myself and was used to the hyperbole of the book business, but it was the novelist's name, Yan Haili, that took my breath away. She was my ex-wife. That brassy bitch—she never stopped vying for attention.

The article, printed in the newspaper's literary and art supplement, gushed that her novel, *Love and Death in September,* was an exotic, whirlwind love story, set by turns in North America, China, Australia, England, Russia, and France. Haili had been working on a potboiler for as long as I'd known her. She'd called it "a fabulous transnational romance." It was yet another project that she hadn't been able to finish. She had never succeeded in finding the center of the story, nor could she connect the various episodes into a plot with a satisfying ending. She had shelved the book again and again, and I'd thought the project was long abandoned. But now—I scanned the article in disbelief—her publisher was claiming the Administrative Office of the Chinese Communist Party had been contacted by the White House, and that President Bush would endorse the English translation of Haili's novel! Why? Because the book "embodied the cooperative spirit between the United States and China in the global war on terrorism." Shoot me if that was true.

The bitch will never change, I realized. I wouldn't let her get away with it this time. I'd figure out a way to expose all her chicaneries and vanity. Even if she begged me on her knees, I wouldn't relent.

"This is nonsense," I said to my boss. "The White House must be more interested in the author than in the book—I mean, in Yan Haili, to find out if she was secretly acting as a Chinese agent."

"That's giving her too much credit," Kaiming said. "She's not smart enough to conduct espionage." He knew how much I hated my ex-wife—that our marriage had lasted only three years before she'd found someone else, and that I couldn't wait to get even with her. He sometimes called Haili "the heartless woman" in front of me.

I said, "So what do you want me to do? This is an arts and culture story—I never write about this kind of thing in my column."

"This time you will. This goes beyond books—I believe it's only one piece of a larger scam."

I was pleased but didn't show it. I said cautiously, "Won't this be a conflict of interest?"

"Conflict of interest? We're dealing with a bunch of scumbags who never do anything by the rules. You can't handle them by acting like a gentleman. I want you to throw all your fire into this case."

"If you want me to expose this scam, you'd better have some idea how it got started."

"I met Jiao Fanping, her publisher, in Beijing last month. Only he's not a true publisher—he's nothing but a profiteer. I want you to write something to expose their scheme before they embarrass lots of us Chinese here in America. We must nip this in the bud."

"I'm afraid it's already blooming into an evil flower."

"We can still pluck it off."

"This will become personal." I tried to smile but felt my face tight.

"I only want you to do the job." My boss smiled.

"I'll see what I can do."

Pleased, Kaiming rose and headed back out to his office, the tail of his pale blue shirt swaying a little. His shoulders were so thick that he appeared to be slightly stooping.

Outside the window, two toddlers were playing noisily in a canary kiddie pool on the neighbors' lawn. It was early September, and still warm. Beyond the lawn were the boxwood hedges, and then a length of flimsy pier that dipped into the edge of Little Neck Bay. In the distance flocks of seabirds sailed through the sky like shattered clouds. A rust-colored tanker lay at anchor, silhouetted against the pale shoreline and the curving belt of the Cross Island Parkway. As I gazed out, I began to think about Kaiming's reasons for assigning me Haili's story, despite my personal involvement. Of the fourteen reporters in our company, GNA (Global News Agency), I was the one known for my exposés, shining a light onto the towering corruption of Chinese politics and media in my regular column. My acid tongue was legendary, my comments heart-stabbing, my views uncompromising, and my predictions sometimes even oracular. Naturally I was hated by officials and celebrities, and cursed by those I'd exposed. Yet when everyday people of the

Chinese diaspora discovered my writing, it was, in their own words, "like discovering a new continent." Most of GNA's readership consisted of Chinese living abroad, but some of my columns made it past the partly erected Great Firewall into the mainland. Here in New York's Chinese community, dignitaries steered clear of me, regarding me as an annoyance best avoided. My boss had probably put me on the case of Haili's "landmark novel" for another, more pragmatic reason: unlike most of the other reporters for our Chinese-language website, I was fluent in English and wouldn't swallow my *a*'s and *the*'s. That would facilitate my investigation of the Americans' involvement in this whole affair. (He knew that the White House's endorsement was a boast.)

I reread the *Yangtze Morning Post* article. When I got to the end, I felt incensed. This was unmistakably the book Haili had been working on all those years, but it had never occurred to me that she would have the temerity to exploit the tragedy of 9/11. According to the article, the book follows a young couple, a princely American man and a bewitching Chinese woman, whose coming honeymoon to Bali is annulled by the groom's disappearance in the collapsed World Trade Center. He'd been in the North Tower. They had just been married the weekend before. The bride, wrecked by her husband's death, almost dies, herself, of grief. For months, wherever she goes, she thinks she can see glimpses of his strapping figure in crowds or at street corners. Sometimes when she picks up the phone, the voice she hears is his. His laughter echoes in her mind and makes her eyes brim with tears. The man had dreamed of becoming a watercolor painter with a studio in Paris, on the willow-lined Seine. How remorseful she is for not having persuaded him to follow his passions! For almost half a year after his death she can't go to work, fearful even of crossing streets and riding elevators. But now, she's finally found the courage to write this book, which is said to be "utterly autobiographical," because she wants to share both her joy and her pain with others.

I knew Haili's current husband, Larry Clements. He was American, but that was about all he had in common with the tragic lover in Haili's book. Just two weeks back I had run into him in front of Lincoln Center, beside the leaping fountains. Larry was an utterly unremarkable-looking man: in his early forties, wide-framed, with an incipient potbelly and a mop of salt-and-pepper hair. I no longer felt the hatred I'd once had for him. I'd come to realize that Haili had married him not because he was the better man, but because she'd been looking for someone who could give her a green card and an auspicious beginning in America. So Larry, a stock analyst on Wall Street with his own office, must have been her ideal catch, and she must have been the seducer, not the other way around. Larry always dressed in a suit and tie. He had expensive taste and was an opera aficionado. A typical petty bourgeois, in my opinion, probably a philistine.

According to the *Post,* Haili had already started promoting her book in China—she'd made several public appearances in Beijing and Shanghai the month before. The article described her as a beautiful, enigmatic young lady from New York, who had "elegant manners," "a lithe figure," "a lovely velvety voice," and "dreaming eyes full of memories." She wore a jade heart necklace (her love charm), which dangled above her fair-skinned cleavage. She emanated grace and culture. "Her whole person, her body language, enunciates the profoundest theme of life: Love! No wonder it's universally agreed that style is the person. In Yan Haili's case, the writer's personal beauty and her gorgeous prose dovetail—I venture to say they enhance and deepen each other." It was reported that Haili had captivated her young audience the moment she began to speak about writing her book, a process that had been so painful and so personal that, talking about it in front of the crowd, she'd had to pause now and again to collect herself. The audience, especially the college students among them, fixed their admiring eyes on her the whole time. Without question, her words had struck a chord in their hearts. Many girls couldn't stop brushing away their tears.

I knew better than anyone else how pretty and charming Haili was. She was a beauty who could make people break off midconversation when she entered a room. But she was certainly not a gifted writer, despite her excellent taste as a reader—she loved magical realism, Agatha Christie, Marguerite Duras, and D. H. Lawrence. ("If I could write a book like *Lady Chatterley's Lover*, I would die happy," she often gushed. Of course, ditto for me.) When we were a young married couple in China, I helped her revise and edit her stories and prose poems, and she submitted them to magazines and contests. Even with my help, she'd seldom succeeded in placing her pieces, much less seeing them in print. Lacking in confidence but ebullient with creative ambition, she adopted a pair of pen names, Quill from Heaven and Azure Dragonfly, as most Chinese writers do, both for self-protection and to show their modesty. Since our divorce, seven years ago, I'd been following her publications, which mostly seemed to be small write-ups, the size of a block of tofu, in community newspapers. She also posted linked stories on her blog, which, I realized now, must have been chapters from her novel. They were embarrassingly amateurish. Her passages were marred with double and triple exclamation marks. She dropped pretentious expressions right and left, calling mung-bean noodles "dragon's beard" and aniseeds "octagonal stars." I used to try to curb this "poetic" impulse of hers, but it had only gotten worse after we parted ways. I couldn't see how she could possibly have developed into a published novelist overnight.

I often wondered what had happened to her youthful wanderlust. Was she still longing to see the world? I doubted it. She was so comfortably ensconced in New York—"the capital of the world," she loved to brag. Back in college in Changchun City, she used to dream of serving as a diplomat, traveling the globe and hopping from country to country. "Every morning you would wake to find a new foreign sun," she'd say. She'd even aspired to become a sort of female Odysseus—a woman who existed only in her interminable wanderings and who wouldn't fear meeting her death in a distant land or even at the bottom of an uncharted sea. When she confided her secret thoughts to me in the aspen grove behind her ceramic-tiled classroom building, I was blown away, never having even thought of stepping foot out of our native Jilin province. Her wild spirit fascinated me and opened a vista in my mind's eye. Yes, yes, I told her, human beings must go anywhere their hearts lead them—our experiences must live up to the passions we are capable of sustaining. So I urged her to pursue her vision, to, in her own words, "build a home in the sky and eventually glitter like a star on a cloudless night."

She worked hard on her English, a subject in which she came out number one of the seventy-eight students of the year 1994 in the music department of her normal university. She said to me, "English means freedom to me. It will give me a pair of strong wings." I agreed, nodding like an idiot.

What had happened to her dreams of liberation, which, to

her, could only be expressed in the English language? Where were her wings? As far as I knew, she had stopped writing in English long ago, seeing more opportunities and a larger readership in China. She claimed that she was now already "free and happy." How true the caveat is: contentment shackles your soul.

Our two editorial assistants, both interns, were unfamiliar with the art and literary scene in China, so I preferred to do the research by myself. I began looking for more press coverage of the novel on China News Service and SINA News. I found that her publisher, Jiao Fanping, had granted an interview to *The Readers' Guide Weekly* a few days before. In it, he claimed that Random House had just purchased the novel for an undisclosed large figure, and that negotiations with major European, Japanese, Latin American, and Taiwanese publishers were all under way. "There's every indication that this extraordinary book will become an international best seller," Jiao avowed. "Just last Friday I heard from Hollywood that they were interested in acquiring the movie rights to this novel. How about that! This is absolutely phenomenal and fantastic, a breakthrough in our country's effort to export our cultural products."

I knew of Jiao Fanping, the only son of a high official in the State Council. Jiao had made his fortune on the Chinese stock market and then started building his own empire, which began with a small publishing house and a few cafés and dumpling joints near college campuses, all in Beijing. In recent years he'd been branching out into the music and movie industries. His statements about Haili's book had to be bald-faced lies. I doubted she had completed the novel yet, let alone shopped it around to foreign publishers. Until the book's actual appearance, she would still belong to the vast army of unpublished novelists.

I went down the hallway to my boss's office. "Kaiming," I said, "the scheme surrounding my ex-wife's novel might be bigger and uglier than we thought."

"That's why I want you to look into it—nobody but you can uncover the whole thing."

"Believe me, no reputable publisher will consider the book seriously. It's just a shallow romance."

"Well, you know in China there's no distinction between a literary novel and a romance novel. All the genres are just lumped together. Most readers can't tell the difference anyway."

"That's true. The Japanese don't make such a distinction either. But still, quality is quality—I don't think any decent publisher here will give Haili's book the time of day."

"You never know. It can be brought out as a romance novel here and then advertised as a literary novel back in China, where they're planning to make most of their money anyway. I want you to expose those frauds."

"You know that I can't help but be biased."

"That's all right—you can use it to your advantage."

Kaiming grinned, baring his square teeth. I had known him long enough to see that he'd wanted to harness my personal feelings for this job all along. He often stressed that we report every major piece of news from a unique perspective. By his definition, "Genius is originality" (which I doubt, because the world is overpopulated with original asses). If GNA kept doing news in a peerless fashion, Kaiming believed, we would become an indispensable source for the Chinese-language media around the globe. He also stressed, "Truthfulness is our only way to survive in this news business and to make money in the long run." He himself specialized in political commentary and most times could predict the developments of current events; his opinions were highly valued, even by some experienced China hands in the States. He was regarded as a walking encyclopedia of Beijing's top political circles, where he had secret sources. He knew how to get things done. In the case of *Love and Death in September,* he seemed to see my feelings about Haili as the most powerful fuel for our investigation.

TWO

Icalled Haili the next morning; she picked up on the seventh
ring. At first her voice was sleepy, but the more she spoke
the more animated it became. That voice! It used to tug my
heartstrings and lace my dreams with messages and meanings,
but now it was businesslike and dismissive. As I started firing
off my questions, I could hear her breathing, seething with fury.
I stayed calm and emphasized that I was calling purely out of
courtesy. I'd been asked to devote one of my columns to the
clamor surrounding *Love and Death in September*.

"Don't presume I enjoy talking with you. It's my job to hear
your side of the story. Can we meet this afternoon?"

After a long pause, she agreed to see me in a café in the Village, where she and Larry lived. I asked that she show me the
manuscript so I could report on it accurately. "If it impresses
me, I'll add my praises to the heap," I told her.

"You're not my editor. Why should I let you see it?"

"If you don't, I'd only be able to repeat what others have
already said. That wouldn't be fair to the book or to you."

"What have you heard?" She sounded anxious. "I didn't mention you in it."

I was taken aback, never having imagined being cast in a story
(though I wouldn't mind if a fine book had me as an endearing
character). I told Haili some of the comments that were already
circulating online. "You should think about the consequences of
publishing this book," I said. "There's a lot of talk already, and

not everything is positive. Once words are in print, there'll be no way to undo them."

"Thanks very much," she said, "for your wisdom."

"Can I take a look at the manuscript?"

She paused again. "All right—I'll show you a couple of chapters."

That would do. I didn't need to eat the entire pig to know what the pork tasted like.

I STILL HATED HAILI. For more than a decade Chinese couples hadn't been allowed to go abroad together, so I couldn't leave China with her. Before coming to the States seven years ago to join her in New York, I had noticed changes in her correspondence, in her phone calls, and wondered if she'd been carrying on with another man. It was said that in America people changed sex partners as often and easily as they changed their diets, that "freedom" included liberty from marital constraints, and that the ultimate purpose of life was to pursue personal happiness at all costs. Tormented by suspicions, I insisted that Haili get me out of China—not only for us, but so that I could have a second chance in life. My career at the state-owned newspaper in Changchun City was faltering: the editor in chief, who was also the vice Party secretary of my work unit, picked on me every chance he got. He told everyone that I had permed my hair like a woman, when in fact it just got curly by itself as it grew longer. The man, a high school dropout, was jealous that I had a BA in journalism from Jilin University and that I was married to such a beautiful woman. He often sounded me out about whether I might leave and, putting on a face like a smiling tiger, would ask me, "When will you head for New York, Danlin? All lights are green—you're free to go anytime."

I knew he wanted to get rid of me and give my job to a relative or friend. So I had to go to the States and join my wife; otherwise I might snap and do something terrible.

After twenty hours of flight I landed at JFK, where Haili was waiting. She looked better than ever. She called a yellow cab and took me directly to a seedy inn in Chinatown, near Little Italy, saying she'd found me a job in a restaurant and I'd better stay within walking distance of it.

"I don't understand," I said, baffled. "Why are we staying here?"

"This is just temporary," she said.

The moment I dropped my suitcases and lay down on the bed to ease my sore back, she handed me a folded envelope that contained a wad of cash, five hundred dollars in mixed bills. She said she had paid a whole month's rent for this place, but she'd have to stay away from me for the time being because she was up to her eyebrows in teaching and administrative work. "Starting is always hard in America," she told me, as if I were a student taking a music lesson from her. "But you're an able man, and I'm sure you'll find your way and make it here. America is a place where hard work can pay off, and with your kind of education and brains, you'll find a professional job. Just be patient and persevere."

She said she had to go and would see me the next day. I was logy from the twelve-hour time difference and couldn't make heads or tails out of what was going on. I got ahold of her arm and pulled her closer so I could have a better look at her and also kiss her. But she broke loose, saying she was having her monthly flow. For now I must rest well, she insisted. After she left, I went out to a diner and had Yangchow fried rice, which tasted better and richer than that sold at food stands back home, thanks to the fresh cooking oil and extra eggs and shrimp. The sweet peas and onion gave it an exotic flavor, but that was all right. I was amazed that they served the rice on a square plate instead of in a bowl. After the meal, I returned to the inn and slept for eleven hours straight.

THE NEXT DAY around noon Haili came again, wearing a scarlet sheath, high heels, heavy makeup, and lilac perfume. She looked like a seductress in a Western, and I came within a breath of suggesting that she don long gloves. No sooner had she sat down than she handed me a glossy blue folder. "Here are our divorce papers," she said, looking away. "Please sign them."

"Why . . . why are you doing this to me?" I stammered, gagging. I could barely get out the words.

"Things change, Danlin, and so does love. I need someone who has strong shoulders, but you've always been like a younger brother to me. Ever since we married, I've taken care of you. I'm tired of it and need someone who can take care of *me*. And so I've met someone else."

"I . . . I still love you," I said, fighting down the sob surging in my throat, though tears, hot and unstoppable, trickled down my cheeks. I turned, grabbed a pillow, and wiped my face with it.

"In that case, you should have my best interests in mind, shouldn't you? Please sign these." She patted the folder in front of me while my grief quickly turned to rage.

I knew it was no use protesting in the moment—I'd need to get my wits together. So I held back my anger and muttered, "I'll think about it."

She placed her attorney's embossed card on the folder, then rose and left. The second the door was closed behind her, I collapsed sobbing. I cried hard, punching the sheet and the blanket and biting the pillows. Never had I expected I would land in such a trap.

I wept on and off for hours, kneeling on the floor with my elbows on the bed. Every object in this "nonsmoking" room gave off a tang of tobacco; even the faded flowery wallpaper smelled acrid, which further stoked my anger—it seemed everything was fake in this so-called Beautiful Land. As I went on sniveling, my face rubbing the sheet and my knees scraping the carpeted floor, dusk was falling outside, the street abuzz with traffic and people. Now and then a car tooted or a truck braked with a screech. Somewhere a siren, probably from a fire engine, squealed.

Finally I climbed up from the floor, blew my nose, and washed my face. My chest was so full that I couldn't think coherently, my temples hammering, so I went out to get a breath of fresh air. I began to think. I would never sign the divorce papers, nor would I let Haili get away without paying for what she'd done to me. I would spread the word about her promiscuity in both New York and Changchun, and make her name stink everywhere—even her parents would feel ashamed to mention their slut of a daughter in the presence of others, and no suitable man would want to marry her younger sister. Yes, no matter how Haili begged me to relent, I would plague her like a disease.

But as I was roaming the streets of lower Manhattan, a numbing pain sank deeper and deeper in me and I began to calm down. I realized if I tried to smear Haili's name, I might also make a fool of myself—I could turn myself into a laughing-stock. People would point at my back when I passed by, shake their heads, and say to others, "If you don't treat your wife well, you too will be made a cuckold."

I leaned over the rail on the Brooklyn Bridge for a long time, watching the glittering flow of the rush-hour traffic on the Manhattan Bridge up the river. These bridges had appeared quite magnificent just the previous evening, when I had viewed them from the descending plane—one stream of red lights going against another stream of white. Now beyond that glowing torrent of traffic, in the indigo sky an airliner was drifting away, wavering like a ghostly lantern. It was windy, and the water below was choppy, shimmering like colossal scales, as though churned by the vibration of the thundering wheels from the bridge. As a blue tugboat chugged past against the current with a little skiff of the same color in tow, I imagined jumping into the East River. But what next? Beyond that I could not visualize a thing. People here wouldn't even notice that one man, healthy and in his prime and full of potential, was missing—a new arrival like myself hadn't even become a number here yet. (Haili had mentioned she had several ID cards.) Unless my body washed ashore, no one would pay me any attention. But fish might eat me up before that could happen. Would Haili grieve over my disappearance? Probably not. Would she bother to look for me or worry about what had become of me? No, unlikely. She'd feel relieved and might not even report the case to the police. Good riddance, she'd think, and continue with her life. Perhaps her memories of me would trouble her for a few weeks, but in time she would wipe me out of her mind. So it would be foolish for me to die here and now, as though of shame or a mental disorder. No, I wouldn't fade out of her life so easily.

It would make no sense to try to save a broken marriage, so I signed the divorce papers a week later. I enrolled in a language school, taking two courses as a full-time student, so that I could stay in America legally. With the help of a former schoolmate, I found a job at a small community newspaper. I quit my classes as soon as my boss began the process of sponsoring me for a green card. Two years later, right after becoming a permanent resident, I moved on to a bigger newspaper despite my boss's reproving me for betrayal. After job-hopping three more times, I landed my current position.

THE CAFÉ in the Village where Haili and I were to meet was somewhat gloomy inside, though a small electric candle glowed in a glass shade on every table. She was already there when I arrived. She lifted her hand, her slim fingers wagging at me, showing a diamond ring. I went over and took the seat opposite her.

"So you're working on me?" she said almost languidly, her long eyes fixed on me.

"Believe me, I'd prefer to spend my time differently, but my boss assigned me this topic. This is nothing personal."

A young waitress wearing frayed jean shorts came over. She kept pushing up the bridge of her oversize glasses as she took my coffee order; she must have been a college student, fresh out of the classroom—her mind seemed elsewhere. Haili was already sipping a double espresso, the dish in front of her still holding the rim of an elephant ear. I was amazed that she'd eaten almost the whole large pastry. She continued, "I do take this personally. After so many years' hard work and frustration, at last I'm making a breakthrough. And you seem determined to ruin it for me, don't you?"

"The only thing that could ruin you would be the poor quality of your work. Nothing but your own blunders can undo you—that's common sense."

"You still can't quit playing the wise guy. But this time, you'd better mind your own business. My novel is a national project, endorsed by the Chinese government."

"Really?" Flummoxed, I needed a moment before I could reply. "Are they bankrolling the project?"

"I'll just say that there're people in high places supporting my book. You're not dealing with me alone."

Like the Party's Central Committee and the White House? I remembered the ridiculous *Post* article and wanted to laugh, but restrained myself. Surely, anything could become a national project if it got some powerful officials interested in it. Despite Haili's composed voice, I sensed the edge of her anger. My temper was simmering too; the old wound was opening in me again, festering and gaping. "To the best of my knowledge," I said, "you started the book several years ago and it had nothing to do with 9/11. It's supposed to be autobiographical. How in God's name did you lose your husband in the World Trade Center? How did Larry became a gorgeous artist?"

"It's a novel, for which I'm free to invent drama and characters. The beauty of fiction writing is that you can create people and episodes to fully realize the story. You can give your own logic and order to the life you dramatize. Sometimes you even must lie in order to tell a bigger truth."

"But the main characters are named after you and Larry, and in your statements to the press you insist that the story is based on your personal experiences, every episode rooted in an actual event. Your claim of absolute authenticity undercuts your artistic license."

"That conceit is part of the novel."

"But fantasies and verbal fireworks don't add up to genuine art. It's always convenient to consume others' suffering," I said, becoming angrier by the second. "When the families of 9/11 victims find out what you've written, what will they think? Won't they accuse you of exploiting their pain and losses? Some might even say you've committed an anti-American act."

"Oh, knock it off. You're so self-righteous, as always." She dismissed my words with a wave of her hand. "You think I wasn't aware of those issues? But my artistic talent is my pass to creative freedom. Besides, lots of people have made good use of the tragedy. Some of Larry's colleagues made fortunes right after 9/11. Practically every capable stockbroker benefited from the attacks."

"That doesn't make it right, what you're doing," I said, unmoved.

"By comparison," she said, and I could see her mind racing, "I'm much more honest than a broker. I have put more than two thousand hours into the novel. The fruit of my labor will do good in the world—it will promote emotional exchange between the Chinese and the Americans and help readers empathize with the victims and their families."

I tipped back my head and laughed. My laughter drew the eyes of the young waitress and of two men seated on high barstools at the counter. I knew that Haili could always come up with some skewed explanation on the spur of the moment. There was no question in my mind that my ex-wife and her publisher meant to deceive the public. Worse yet, her novel was cheap, shoddy, and, according to what was reported, full of gushing expressions and schlock. But I couldn't press her anymore, as much as I wanted to, because I needed to get ahold of the portion of the manuscript she had promised me.

I told her, "I'll be fair when I write about your book."

"Danlin, you're a gentleman." She dropped her voice a little and peered at me, tiny sparks flitting in her eyes. "I can trust you on this one, can't I?"

"I can't promise anything at this moment, but like I said, I'll be impartial."

"Then I'll owe you one." She smiled, her cheeks going pink.

For Haili, that could range from a dinner in an upscale restaurant to a pair of opera tickets. She always assumed that she could handle me easily. Annoyed, I wanted to tell her to put away her old charms, but I merely said, "Can I have the pages?"

She opened her quilted tote bag, which had a brass zipper on either side, obviously made by cheap Chinese labor, and she took out a sheaf held by a red clamp, more than a hundred pages thick. "These are some chapters, self-contained more or less. Of course, after the book is edited, it will be in better shape. So don't be so nitpicky." She lifted her hand and tucked a loose strand of hair behind her ear. Then she pressed her fingers on her hoop earring, a thick jade bangle sliding down her arm, and tilted her head a fraction to observe me, her eyes gleaming.

"At this point, like I said, I can be fair. Thanks a lot for this." I dropped the pages into my canvas shoulder bag.

"How's Katie?" she asked.

"She's fine." It alarmed me that she'd brought up my girl-friend. Perhaps their paths had crossed recently, but Katie hadn't mentioned anything. What was Haili up to?

"Give her my greetings," she said.

"I shall."

"When are you two going to marry?" A shadow of a smile rose on her high-cheekboned face.

I couldn't tell if it was a genuine question or mockery. Haili must have known I no longer cared about marriage and that I had accepted my bachelor's life. Nevertheless, I found myself saying, "We plan to have our wedding next summer. By then Katie will have finished her book and be ready for tenure."

"Don't forget to invite me and Larry."

"Of course."

I thought of asking after Larry but checked myself, know-ing that their marriage wasn't at all as smooth as it appeared. They often fought, I'd heard. Rumor had it that Haili would call

Larry names even in front of her guests, because she spoke to them in Chinese, which he couldn't understand. Not knowing even a little bit of the language, he could only scan others with a vacant face as they giggled and chattered.

I stood and took my leave, glad to have Haili's pages in my bag.

THREE

Although I'd told Haili that I was planning a wedding, there were no such plans, because I was not interested. Once bitten by a snake, you dread even the sight of a piece of rope lying in grass, but traumatized as I might have been, I was not as scarred as my sister believed. She had warned that I would be unable to fall in love with another woman for the rest of my life. I laughed that off as a cliché. I was of the opinion that many marriages just covered deceptions and betrayals with the veneer of respectability. In theory, the marital bond is supposed to guarantee love without derailment, but in reality love rarely becomes an obligation. As fond as Katie and I were of each other, I avoided the topic of engagement. Fortunately, she wasn't marriage-oriented either, and seemed content with things the way they were.

Katie Torney, the daughter of an Irish father and a Dutch-Filipina mother, was born in golden California and raised in verdant, luxuriant Georgia and South Carolina. Despite her green eyes and long auburn hair, she called herself Asian American, as if her quarter of Filipina blood was what defined her ethnically. This is something I haven't been able to figure out about America, where merely a few drops of black blood can make a person black or biracial, whereas in China people don't care how mixed your blood is or what color your skin is—you are just a Chinese if you've lived long enough among Chinese. Of course, if you are an ethnic minority, you are a converted barbarian, cultured now. Secretly, though, despite my dislike of racism, in the back of my mind there lurked a measure of vanity in dating Katie, who, with her creamy skin and Irish last name, could pass for a white American woman. Haili, after all, had dumped me for a white American man.

An assistant professor of sociology at NYU, Katie specialized in Chinese society and culture. She had been working on a book on the provision of medical services in China's countryside; it was a project she'd have to complete for her tenure evaluation the next fall. To her, it felt like a matter of life and death— a turning point that could make or kill her career. Before the evaluation, she'd have to get the manuscript accepted by a reputable publisher, ideally a major university press. The pressure of her tenure schedule made her anxious and at times distracted. She would come to see me in Flushing once a week; sometimes I'd go to the Village and stay over at her place, usually on weekends. I had suggested moving in together, so that I could have her sleeping beside me every night, but she said she had to concentrate on her research and writing for now. She promised that once she finished her book, she would seriously consider my suggestion. It was unlikely that she'd give up her four-room apartment subsidized by the university, so at best, she'd ask me to move in with her, which would suit me fine—I would happily live near NYU to attend the lectures and talks there.

For years after my divorce, I had withdrawn into myself and hadn't dated anyone. If the tide of lust waxed, I would masturbate over one of Haili's photos taken when she'd been a chaste sophomore or junior, though every time I'd feel sicker afterward. I was afraid of women, especially those from mainland China. God help me, how those females with clenched faces gave me chills! How tough and heartless they could be! Many of them, especially those over forty, were still Red Guards at heart, in awe of neither heaven nor earth. (I'm sure that some of them would rip out my tongue if they could, for the crack I once made in an editorial, "A pot of tea a day keeps China away." The notion that I could abandon our motherland at will, as long as I had my daily tea, was enough to make them see red.)

To subdue my anxieties, I took refuge in work, putting in a lot of overtime. Whether because of that or for other reasons, I soon developed ED. When I woke in the morning, my habitual erection was gone—dead and useless. I began longing for a full-blooded wet dream that might signify something of my manhood regained. But even after I had reduced my work hours, my hard-on refused to return. I tried sea horses, ginseng, deer antler, six-flavor boluses, wolfberries, all bought at an herbal pharmacy in downtown Flushing, but nothing helped. Terrified, I went to an underground brothel, hoping desperately that a paid woman could help me recover. A voluptuous young woman led me into a half-lit room, where a Mongolian folk song, complete with galloping horses' hooves, rapid drumbeats, and the tinkle of the xylophone, droned on. She was from Sichuan, as her accent showed, and was eager to please, but her eagerness made me all the more anxious and unable to get hard. In a giggly voice she urged me to kick back and just enjoy it. She called me "younger brother," though my thirtieth birthday had just slipped by— I was at least three or four years older than she. True, I looked younger than my age, but her term of endearment disabled me altogether, because "younger brother" might have been referring to my dick. She said, "Younger brother can't get up because he's depressed. It's no big deal. Lots of men had this problem but fully recovered after a couple visits to me. I'll take good care of you." I didn't know what to make of that and became even more helpless. As a final resort, she gave me a hand job and told me to come see her again, at least twice a month—next time she'd give me a big discount, she promised.

Afterward the dull pain in my lower back grew deeper, more numbing, and more paralyzing. I feared I might develop a kidney problem. Yet, however restless with stirrings I became, I wouldn't go to a brothel again.

As time went on, I ventured to date a few women—a Korean, a Taiwanese, a Singaporean—but they all left me within two or three months, saying they couldn't figure me out or tolerate the fact that I would never let my guard down. In their eyes, I was an iconoclast who despised his own culture. (To them, the fact that I didn't love dim sum, kung pao chicken, calligraphy, martial arts, Ping-Pong, acupuncture, or the Monkey King—in spite of his magic, which enables him to morph into seventy-two things and creatures—meant I hated China. In the case of the Korean woman, even though I liked kimchi, she still thought me spiteful. But I love only what touches my heart! Who's to say that Brahms did not compose his symphonies also for me?) To make matters worse, they all expected me to propose, as if I had knocked them up and was condemned to a shotgun wedding. I told them I was not interested in marriage and that, at any rate, I didn't have the resources to start a family. One of them insisted that any man dating a woman without the intention of marrying her was a leech, if not a predator. They all accused me of being a "misogynist" (somehow they knew this English word) and of being too calculating—"a big planner," in the words of the Taiwanese woman, a dance teacher with a lovely figure and velvety eyes. Honest to God, I had never harbored any secret plan or taken advantage of them. Yet the more they complained, the more nervous and incapable I became.

Katie had come into my life by chance. I often marveled at my luck. Or was this a gift bestowed on me by Providence for some good deeds done by my ancestors? She was an aspiring China scholar and had some connections in mainland China as well as in Taiwan, Hong Kong, and Southeast Asia. Our first encounter was at the local farmers' market in Flushing, where I used to go shopping. She'd been trying to haggle with a fruit seller but couldn't understand his Cantonese. I helped a little, and then we fell into conversation in Mandarin. Eager to practice the language more often, she agreed to meet again.

On our first coffee date, a week later, we conversed about a variety of topics, from the water shortages in Chinese cities to the lives of the Native Americans on reservations, from European leeks and cucumbers to broccoli, which the first President Bush hated but which had nevertheless begun to be grown in China just a decade earlier as the "green cauliflower." We sat in a café in Washington Square. She was drinking coffee while I had tea, which was too bland for my taste. American teas all tasted artificial and weak to me then. Toward the end of our date, she wanted another coffee and asked if I would like something too. At the time I hadn't developed a taste for coffee yet, but I said, "Coffee's okay." I thought it would be rude not to get anything.

She asked again, "What size?"

"Any size is fine."

She brought back two medium coffees. I took a tiny sip but didn't like it and didn't touch it again. We chatted for a few more minutes before I had to head back to Flushing. As we left, I dropped my coffee into a trash can. Katie looked puzzled and stared at me, her eyes flashing. We said good-bye, and she strolled away toward Eighth Street, her legs muscular with long calves. That night I got an angry message from her—she said I had been inconsiderate and had wasted her money. She wrote: "If you didn't want coffee, you should not have let me buy it for you in the first place. You might call me stingy. Yes, I am stingy. It was my money, which no one else was entitled to waste."

I was blindsided—why would she be so angry over a cup of coffee? She was a professor and must make a decent salary. On second thought, though, I began to feel ashamed. She was right that I should not have just dumped the coffee. If converted into yuan, $1.75 wasn't a trifling amount and could buy two large bowls of noodles in China. I apologized to Katie and said I appreciated her candor. Afterward I still felt uneasy and kept pondering what had prompted me to act so thoughtlessly. As a kind of soul-searching, I wrote a column titled "A Cup of Coffee." In it I asked myself why, poor as I was, I could have been so wasteful, and just as I was trying to make a good impression on a beautiful woman. My answer was that I must still carry some mental residue from my former journalist job in China. Back there, reporters were considered VIPs by the common people and were well treated by the officials at the lower levels, though of course to our bosses we were merely scribes. When I went down to local cities and counties to write about events and people, I almost never paid for food. I always got wined and dined—the local cadres treated me like an official inspector of sorts so that I could put in favorable words about them and their fiefdoms. Even back at my newspaper's office, we paid a pittance of two yuan for our daily staff lunches, which were always lavish and worth at least twenty times more. Many state-owned companies did this, offering their employees lunch essentially for free. As a result, I had grown careless about food and drinks and often threw leftovers away. Indeed, one can always be generous with others' money, I realized. My essay ended with this sentence: "From now on I had better treat every cup of coffee or tea as something bought on my own dime."

The column was well received and got reprinted in several Chinese-language newspapers and magazines in the States and

Canada. Though I'd made no mention of Katie's name in it, I sent her a copy. She liked it and wrote back, saying I was an honest man and she wanted to meet again.

We started seeing each other more often. Katie was three years younger than me, but more experienced in dating. At the very beginning she made it clear that she was not considering a permanent relationship because she wasn't sure how long she could live in New York. That was all the better for me. She said she was attracted to me partly because I was the first man who hadn't made advances to her at the outset of our dating. It was true that I never got ahead of myself. Later, when we did go to bed together, I was a bundle of nerves and couldn't make love to her. I flattered her and made excuses, saying that her body dazzled me. (In a way, that was true—she spent serious time at the gym and was in fantastic shape.) She knew I was lying, but she was patient and said I was all right and there was nothing to be anxious about. I wasn't that bad, she assured me; she'd once dated a guy in his mid-thirties who was already addicted to Viagra (a drug I'd never tried). Feeling less pressure, I began to be able to take it easy.

Little by little, the coldness in me thawed. With Katie I felt as if I were making love for the first time. With her I learned how to use my body to please a woman, how to enjoy being touched and aroused, and how to take possession of her and be possessed. At long last, I could rise to the climax slowly and could relax even though she got into full swing. She awoke the animal in me. For that—for the fact that I finally could feel at ease with my body—I would always be in her debt, no matter where our relationship led us.

KATIE CAME to my place soon after seven p.m., wearing a sweaterdress over black tights. Her handbag was filled with a stack of Chinese articles. She knew the language, having studied it at Johns Hopkins as an undergraduate, but she couldn't read it very fast. Usually she asked me to look through a bunch of articles first and weed out those that wouldn't be useful for her research. She put her bag on the dining table and hugged me. We kissed long and hard, and I started getting an erection. She patted at my crotch; I smiled but stepped back, nodding toward the sizzling pan on the stove.

I always did the cooking for both of us. At the beginning of our relationship, I'd told her about how Haili once misinformed Chinese readers in an article, claiming that if an American man cooked for his woman, that meant he was inadequate in bed. Katie laughed and said she'd always dated men who took pride in their culinary skills. It was better for everyone—domesticity was not her strong suit. When there was no man in her life to do the cooking, she picked up sandwiches from delis or ordered takeout or ate in restaurants. By Chinese standards you could say she was a bit extravagant, but what balanced it out was that she wasn't picky. When we ate out, we could go anywhere: noodle joints, pizzerias, dumpling houses, McDonald's, Subway, even the dingy provincial-food stalls in the basement of Golden Mall on Main Street.

I was cooking beef noodles tonight, mixed with diced asparagus and scallions. When the food was ready, we ate unhurriedly. Katie was in a sour mood because the Chinese consulate had again rejected her visa application. She was known as a minor activist among China scholars here, and two years ago she had helped a group of Tibetans organize an international conference at NYU. Afterward, she wrote an article on China's minority policies for *Harper's Magazine*. She was quite critical of the policies and argued that China had made a great step backward in that area (the police often detained or incarcerated activists without charge). The article got Katie in trouble with the Chinese officials here. One of them told her bluntly at a party: "We have been keeping an eye on you. Don't assume you can get away with your hostility against China. We don't forget. We can ruin your career or help you make it." Indeed, they had crippled, if not destroyed, a good number of scholars by isolating them professionally, by barring them from entering China, even by boycotting them at conferences. Seeing such tactics was what had prompted some China hands years ago, in both Europe and the States, to advise their governments not to criticize China for its reprehensible human rights record. Just do business with the Chinese and make as much money as you can, they argued. Once capitalism has taken root in that country, a strong middle class will emerge and democracy will be on its way. Now we all know that China, the wayward dragon, has grown into an anomaly, an unprecedented combination of one-party oligarchy and rapacious capitalism.

"Did they give you any reason this time?" I asked Katie about her visa application.

"No, the man in the office just told me, 'You know why we must turn you down again.'" She frowned; thin wrinkles creased her forehead, making her heart-shaped face appear gaunt. "Maybe I shouldn't have told them I planned to do field-work in Henan province."

"Do you think that might make them more determined to stop you?"

"Hard to say."

"Did you mention you wanted to interview country folks infected with HIV?"

"No! I'm not that stupid."

"I'll ask Kaiming to put in a word for you," I said. "He must have connections in the consulate."

"Please do." Her eyes warmed a bit.

I began to tell her about the new story I was investigating. Katie had already heard about *Love and Death in September*— the hype had reached the Chinese-language media in the diaspora. She had also seen a short article about it in *China Watch,* a free tabloid distributed only in Chinese stores and on street corners, but she'd had no idea that my ex-wife was the author. I told her about my meeting with Haili and how she had claimed that the novel was "a national project."

Katie smiled and said, "That woman is outrageous."

"To be fair, I don't think she could come up with such an elaborate scheme by herself. She isn't that complicated a person and doesn't have a lot of strategies. So maybe she's right—maybe she does have a clique behind her. But why are they using 9/11 as a selling point?"

"To break into the U.S. book market," Katie said.

"But why?"

"Books are expensive here and she wants to make more money."

"There might be more to it."

"What?"

"I can't put my finger on it. Kaiming said the publisher meant to make most of their money in the Chinese market, so the foreign publication of the book might serve as validation."

"Validation of what?"

"Of its quality."

"That's perverse. Now even a Chinese romance novel needs foreign validation?"

"A lot of fiction readers there don't believe the domestic hype—they're so used to it. But if a novel gains an international reputation, that gets more attention."

After dinner, Katie put on an album by her favorite punk

band, Propagandhi, and began to do the dishes, while I looked through the articles she'd brought along. I found only three that seemed like they would help her with her research. After that, I lounged in a chair and started reading Haili's manuscript. The narrative voice was breezy and for the most part read quickly, but there were also moments when the writing was clunky and vulgar. The narrator, named Yan Haili, emphasized again and again that what she was telling was absolutely autobiographical. She name-dropped at every opportunity, claiming that she'd met a rather scattered list of celebrities: Saul Bellow, Archbishop Desmond Tutu, Sandra Bullock, Hillary Clinton, Laura Bush. One luminary I was certain Haili had once taken a photo with was the Dalai Lama, but she made no mention of him for fear of the censorship in China. She presented herself as a daughter of two distinguished artists, a sculptor and a landscape painter, who had emigrated from Tianjin to Melbourne in the late 1970s, when she was a toddler. She had grown up abroad, she wrote, and was utterly savvy about the Western way of life. But she had also preserved her roots in Chinese culture, which nourished her life and art. That was why she'd kept writing in our beloved native language. She could easily have written this novel in English, she boasted, but she wanted to share her experiences with Chinese readers first. More fundamentally, she had to retain her allegiance to our beautiful, profound, infinitely intricate mother tongue, in which she could frolic and dance at will. Therefore, wherever she went, the Chinese language was her only valuable luggage, her "inexhaustible cornucopia."

The whole tall tale, in a way, was in keeping with Haili's personality. It was a familiar routine to me, and now that I knew what I was dealing with, it didn't bother me too much. What did appall me were the novel's ridiculous sex scenes, in one of which the narrator described her husband's hips at length, calling them "milky in color and perfect in shape and size, as if sculpted by a master artist."

I read the passage out loud to Katie. She laughed, then stepped behind me and wrapped her arms around my neck. "Time for bed," she whispered.

I was always eager to go to bed with Katie. Sometimes after sex, I'd be awash with desire again before daybreak. Tonight I woke up shortly afterward, but my mind was preoccupied with the remaining chapters of Haili's novel. Katie was sound asleep, her breath whistling faintly. I gently extracted myself from her arms, slid out of bed, and walked softly into the living room. Sprawled on the sofa, I went back to Haili's manuscript. The story was getting stranger by the page. The heroine, heartbroken over the loss of her husband, ran into a husky Australian on a flight home to Melbourne. She and the Aussie, a kind of double of her lost husband, fell for each other at first sight. They sneaked into the plane's lavatory and made love there. The narrator described it in relentless detail—the various positions, the maddening but fulfilling act that culminated in multiple orgasms. She confessed, "Walking back up the aisle. I felt my legs buckle as though he were still deep inside me, and my head were about to burst. . . . Even after I returned to my seat, I still felt his kisses all over me—on my earlobes, on my neck, on my nipples, and down below. My mouth and tongue ached from our kissing, while my heart was flooded with pain and ecstasy. Oh, I was teetering between life and death!" With that Haili ended the chapter titled "Romance in the Air."

"Bullshit!" I snorted, wondering how I should approach my article. I was sure that no serious publisher in the West would acquire such a simpleminded book, but why had Haili written it in the first place? And why were the Chinese media pushing it so hard? The novel seemed to be targeted at teenage girls who dreamed of having foreign men ("princes riding white horses") as their future husbands. But even if their marketing succeeded and their sales skyrocketed, it was unheard of to celebrate a sentimental fledgling writer as a literary star.

FOUR

I didn't go into the office the next day—I worked at home instead. On Xinhua, Tencent news, and also the official site of Chinese Writers' Association, I found more about Haili's novel. Hype seemed to be gathering steam in the Chinese media. A long article in the *Journal of Literature and Art* by a critic named Gu Bing declared the publication of *Love and Death in September* a major event in contemporary Chinese literature. It was poised to become an international best seller, he wrote, one that would throw open the doors to the American and European book markets for other Chinese writers. It was part of a new genre that blurred the distinction between fiction and nonfiction, its vividness and authenticity enhanced by raw and stunning photographs. More important, with its fearless and sophisticated protagonist, the novel introduced into today's fiction a new breed of young Chinese woman: one who took migration as the human-historical condition; one who moved around following nothing but her passions while aspiring to a physical and spiritual harmony in her personal life; one who, unlike the majority of the Chinese, who were unable to travel abroad, was absolutely cosmopolitan and multilingual, mingling effortlessly with people of all cultures, feeling at home on all continents. As China was opening its doors fully and more people could go abroad, surely more female characters of this kind would appear in both fiction and nonfiction. Above all, this extraordinary novel celebrated the endurance and universality of human emotions, untrammeled by cultural and linguistic boundaries. As a critic, Gu said he must take off his hat to the deceptively fragile debut author, whose mighty pen had at one stroke secured her a permanent position in Chinese letters.

Who was this Gu Bing? I wondered. Another drooling fraud? Then I remembered the name—I had read about him a few years before. He was the editor in chief of *People's Arts,* a print monthly magazine that boasted a circulation of 140,000 copies and was one of the few Chinese arts periodicals to pay its contributors well. A notorious quote was attributed to him: "I am the standard of your arts." He had said that to a young choreographer in private, but the outraged woman had spilled it publicly. A critic of Gu's power and stature could indeed make or break an artist. But why was he so involved in Haili's book? Did he also have a hand in this scam? Had Haili been carrying on with him? It was possible. She had degenerated into one of those social butterflies, hovering in literary circles, willing to do anything to get their writing published.

As I continued to sort through my search results, I came across a report on a celebratory gathering that had been held in a hotel in downtown Beijing the previous afternoon. It was a news conference of sorts, presided over by Gu Bing and attended by a dozen or so well-known critics, half of whom were professors of contemporary literature. They each spoke to praise the novel and its young author, who must have been inspired by a magnificent vision and a burning ambition. They confessed that they'd been impressed, stunned, even moved to tears. One proclaimed her book "a triumph"; another, "a masterpiece written in iridescent prose, destined to last"; a third, "a majestic work of globalized fiction"; a fourth, "a book of sui generis beauty, poetry, depth, and complexity"; a fifth said it had "transcended personal grief and reached the commonality of human fate"; a sixth raved, "Imagine, four hundred pages without a single false note. As a fellow novelist, I am utterly bowled over. What a splendid debut! Bravo!"

I couldn't conjure up the sublime literary terrain in which these scholars had placed the novel. On what grounds could they call it a "landmark" book? Some of them I knew personally— they'd been sane and modest, and I would never have dreamed that they would join in such false rhapsody. They must have been paid handsomely for their lavish words. With enough money, you can hire the devil to scrub your feet and wash your underwear.

Gu, whose photograph on the website of *People's Arts* showed a balding head, hooded eyes, and a heavy-boned face, declared that translations of this novel were already under way and that soon it would be published "in more than thirty languages simultaneously"—I did a double take, thinking the number might be a typo, but thirty it was—"in nearly forty countries." Gu continued, "This is a tremendous boost to the dwindling reading culture, like a timely rain falling on thirsty fields."

I shook my head in disbelief. It was as if today was these critics' last day on earth and they no longer cared what people would say about them tomorrow. Still, they had families. What would their children and spouses think of them?

I called my boss and reported my findings. "Gu Bing is another crook," Kaiming said.

"You know him?" I asked.

"I met him in Beijing three weeks ago."

"Why are they doing this? To commemorate 9/11?" I couldn't contain my sarcasm.

"For money. They want to make a huge profit, so the book must stand out among thousands of novels published in China this year."

"But it's a piece of crap. I read parts of it last night."

"See, that's why I put you on the case. I figured nobody but you could get access to the manuscript." Kaiming chuckled.

"What's going on between Gu Bing and Yan Haili?"

"Gu is her editor. I forgot to mention him to you."

"But . . . I thought he just edited his arts magazine."

"He's been working for Jiao Fanping's publishing house on the side. He can't wait to see Haili's novel become an international best seller so he can have his share of the profit. He already told me he was planning to use the money for down payments on a Volkswagen Jetta and an apartment on the outskirts of Beijing."

"I can't believe he's planning to get rich this way."

"Gu said he and the author had agreed to split the royalties, half and half."

"Can I mention his plan in my column?"

"No, no, you'd better not or Gu Bing will surmise I told you that. It would be unprofessional to quote your boss. Frankly, if it was a good book, I wouldn't give a shit about how they promote it."

"But we started the investigation and will publish our report. There's no way you can stay clear of this."

"We report it because we must prevent those crooks from putting on a spectacle here. Besides, they've been misleading Chinese people and making it look like China and the U.S. are similar."

"I agree. Inside China they can bamboozle heaven and earth into trading places, and perhaps no human being can stop them there. But why would they bring all of their lies here?"

"Through New York the book can enter the world market. There are only four or five gateways for writers in China to go through if they want to gain an international readership. Paris is the French gateway, Berlin the German gateway, London and New York the English gateways. The Big Apple is by far the widest gateway. Only through one of these entrances can writers from a non-Western language break onto the international scene. In your ex-wife's case, they picked New York as their point of entry."

"Where did you get the gateway idea?"

"I figured it out by myself."

Kaiming was a sharp fellow from Shaoshan, the town where Mao Zedong was born—because of this, some people had dubbed him "Chairman Mao's grandnephew." But he was much handsomer than the great leader—he had dark features, bright eyes, a strong, straight nose, and a slightly cleft chin, which often made me think that if I were him I'd have grown a beard. Kaiming was a gifted entrepreneur: he had come to the States with only six hundred dollars seventeen years before, and now he owned a substantial part of our agency. Even the Chinese consulate here respected him. He was invited to all the major public events in the Asian communities in D.C. and New York. His personal networks spanned the world: he had connections from South Africa to Finland. Before hanging up, I mentioned Katie's visa application. Kaiming said he'd bring it up with an official at the consulate.

In the afternoon I continued to research the novel and think about my angle. It was obvious to me that Haili was hand in glove with her publisher and editor, but for now I needed to stick to the evidence I had. As I was about to start the first paragraph of my report, my phone rang. It was Haili, who sounded anxious.

I told her I couldn't ignore the lies she had multiplied, and that I had to do my job. "To be frank," I said, "I cannot figure out why you would claim that your lightweight romance novel is a literary masterpiece."

"Don't be such a prig," she shot back. "When *Jane Eyre* was first published, it was considered a romance. So was *Gone with the Wind*. Even *Anna Karenina* was a kind of romance novel, wasn't it? There's no reason for maintaining a literary hierarchy in our times."

"That's beside the point. The question is whether you have written as important a book as you claim."

"I knew it—I knew you'd find a way to get even with me."

"Let's be fair. If your book were actually important, you'd be entitled to promote it any way you want, and even I might sing your praises. But it's terrible—it made my skin crawl. How could you describe a black girl's eyes as being 'as pretty and fresh as iced Coca-Cola'? How on earth could you compare Larry's butt to a masterpiece of sculpture? Honestly, I don't think his ass can be that gorgeous. It's really beyond me. To top that, you seemed—"

"Stop attacking me! It's fiction, understand? You can't match everything in the story with real life like you can find a seat with a ticket in an opera house."

"But in the book and in your interviews you emphasized time and again that the novel is thoroughly autobiographical, that every episode is factual, and that you even lost your virginity to your American husband. Was *that* true?" I stopped and closed my eyes. I remembered the night of our wedding—I had gotten drunk from nerves and had thrown up in our newly painted bedroom. Haili had cleaned up the mess without a word and then stirred vinegar and honey into a bowl of boiled water for me.

"Danlin, are you still there?" Haili asked.

"Yes."

"You know I still have a soft spot for you. Can we meet somewhere and talk more about this?"

"What do you mean?"

"Didn't you used to insinuate that you'd love to spend time with me?"

"That was before I met Katie."

"Can we spend a night together? I'll be free tonight and tomorrow night, and I'll be good to you."

"I see." I pretended to think about it. "Where's Larry?"

"He's in Mexico City for a conference."

"You know, I had the most amazing sex with Katie last night. Oh, you can't imagine how good she is in bed. She has such beautiful hips."

Silence followed.

Then Haili said, "I know you're my enemy. If you're resolved to rock our boat, we'll have to sink you first."

"That's fine. Suit yourself."

"I warn you not to interfere with our business. The novel is a national project. My publisher's parents have infinite pull in China and can ruin you and your family."

"They may rule heaven and earth there, but not in the United States of America. You know it was a bunch of journalists who brought down Richard Nixon. But even if Jiao Fanping's parents ruled the White House, I would still do what my profession asks of me."

"You'll have hell to pay."

"I hear you. Bye now."

I hung up. I had waxed idealistic over the phone, but practically speaking I could afford to stick my neck out on this story because my parents were retired. I had only them and an older sister back in China, and she didn't work outside her home. There was little that Haili and her collaborators could do to hurt them. In addition, by her own confession, Haili *loved* my parents—she had even visited them two years ago, when she returned to China on business. They were still unaware of our divorce—we had agreed to spare them the heartache. Haili still called them Mom and Dad, and I knew she had just mailed them two bottles of amino acids. She had also sent them a box of peppered beef jerky before the last Spring Festival. I didn't believe that Haili would ever actually turn on my parents, who still adored her and praised her to high heaven in front of anyone who would listen.

I had another trump card unknown to Haili. I'd just been naturalized, and I no longer had to obey the Chinese officials here or fear that they might revoke my passport. At the moment I held no passport. I had sent my old one to the Chinese consulate for renewal a couple of months ago and hadn't gotten it back yet. I had surrendered my green card to the INS at the naturalization ceremony, so legally I was in transition from Chinese to American citizenship. The United States recognizes dual citizenship but discourages it; China absolutely does not accept it. I understood their mind-set—on paper, I knew loyalty ought to remain undivided, though in my heart I sometimes felt torn, nagged by doubts about giving up my Chinese citizenship, even stung by something close to grief. Yet to survive, I had to break away, to find space where I could live safely and freely. Freedom and equality were precious enough to me that I was willing to go through the pain of uprooting myself. I had mailed in my citizenship certificate and a photo that showed both ears for a U.S. passport—I expected to receive it in a month or so. Although Haili's threat was by no means idle, I believed that in America, as long as I paid my taxes and obeyed the law, the state would protect me.

FIVE

I finished my column the next morning, and our website posted it, as usual, in the early afternoon. Within hours, our notification system signaled that the piece had been linked to sites in Hong Kong, Taiwan, and Europe. In the article I held up the shoddy reality of Haili's novel against the image of the brilliant tour de force projected by her publisher, quoting several of the book's most egregious passages to make my point. I revealed the illicit business connections between the author, the editor, and the publisher, saying, "The book is a brainchild of this troika, who intend to exploit people's memories of 9/11, swindle them out of their money, and get rich overnight."

Because the anniversary of the tragedy was just around the corner, my article got a lot of attention. Many community newspapers in North America asked GNA for permission to reprint it, and the next day our phone rang continuously. Some callers were ordinary people giving leads to other exploitative business deals in their communities—they'd had no recourse before, but now they hoped we would investigate. On the entertainment sites of SINA and Tencent, people condemned Yan Haili and Jiao Fanping and Gu Bing, calling them "an evil triangle" and "a gang of three." A number of readers insisted that Haili must have given favors to that shameless editor in chief, who was said to be a notorious womanizer. "She must be Gu Bing's mistress and a social climber," one person wrote. Another joined in, "The three must be a ménage à trois." Some photos, not only of the three of them but also of some critics present at the news conference about the novel, were posted online as a roster of the shameless. I allowed myself a small, private moment of triumph. Everything indicated that the scam might be falling apart.

But within days, positive articles about Haili's book again began to appear in China, both in newspapers and on websites like Xinhua Readers and Chinawriter. *The Guangzhou Daily* ran a new interview that showed a photo of her on a cruise boat on the Hudson River: she was wearing tea-colored sunglasses, her long beige skirt fluttering in the breeze, and her hair was slightly tousled. She looked elegant and at ease, an exemplar of a young woman who had made it abroad. She had been born into such wealth, she declared in the interview, that she had "no concept of money," which to her was somewhat like noodles growing on trees—she didn't know where it came from. She had never worked a single day in her life (though actually she'd been a teacher at a New York prep school for years) and didn't value material possessions at all—she called herself "a spiritual aristocrat." Yet what she was utterly passionate about was love—pure, unconditional, everlasting love. Love was her religion and her god—for this alone she'd been born and would be happy to die. She had started her writing career, she claimed, by composing love letters every day in her early teens. She slipped them into the book bags of the smart boys she liked. I snorted out loud when I read that—she'd never once written me a love letter. It was I who had kept writing to her, serenading her on paper so as to push aside another boy who was after her. It was true that she had always idolized talented young men, especially if they were artistic—aspiring poets, novelists, painters, composers—but when we were growing up she didn't know many such geniuses (as she called them). She once told me that I was the smartest fellow she'd ever met. Of course, after coming to New York, she encountered all sorts of brilliant men, many of them able to outshine me with bigger egos and stronger drive. Her genius pool expanded, and so did her sense of herself.

How had she degenerated into such a shameless liar? Was it because I had failed her, because I hadn't lived up to her expectations? I don't think so. Never had I promised her I'd become an artist or poet. She had often railed against me for lacking ambition, but no one can develop more than his potential allows. What can you do if you were born an everyman?

But there was more. To my astonishment, *The Yangtze Morning Post* reported that Haili had just sold her movie script, which she'd adapted from the novel, to Panorama Pictures in Hollywood—for a whopping $1.3 million. This was the largest cultural export ever accomplished by an individual Chinese author, the article claimed, and in fact, Haili had made history. "They love the script," she told the reporter. "The movie director and his colleagues read it with tears in their eyes."

As a final touch, her editor, Gu Bing, revealed to the *Post* that the English translation of the novel had just been finished by the foremost American translator of Chinese works, Edward Silverwood.

I was puzzled by Haili's audacity. She and her collaborators weren't hesitating to further their scheme, ignoring my article and the public outcry, as if all the uproar had not put the slightest dent in their plans. If anything, they were pushing even harder. Their lies seemed to be coming at me faster than I could absorb them—now there was an announcement in *The Readers' Guide Weekly* that a Chinese literary association in New Jersey, the Nobel Prize Nomination Committee in North America, would be nominating Yan Haili for the Nobel Prize in literature. I laughed in disbelief. I knew that group—it was chaired by the owner of a Cantonese restaurant and composed of some twenty self-styled literary buffs, every one of them with a pen name like Summer Rain, Smoky Eyes, Little Bamboo, or Ink Eater. They were deadly serious in their mission to spread appreciation of contemporary Chinese literature worldwide, and they concentrated their efforts on various uncommon channels. They ran a micropress that brought out six or seven titles a year by immigrant authors. Whenever a Chinese writer or an official of cultural affairs passed through New Jersey, the group would host him or her in their chairman's restaurant and then post photos online as a boast—in fact, they feared that the world might have forgotten them. They helped Chinese writers send signed copies of their books to major U.S. universities, whose names would be paraded on the authors' résumés as collectors of their works. In return, members of the group would be invited to writers' conferences and literary festivals held at tourist resorts in China, where they would stuff themselves at banquets and get lost while trying to sightsee. They'd also speak at Chinese college campuses as figures of success: people who had made money and a name for themselves in North America, that wild, awesome land.

How could they be qualified to nominate someone for the Nobel Prize? A legitimate nominator must be at least a full professor or a scholar of some repute. Moreover, the prize is not for a single book but for lifetime achievement. (In one critic's snide remark, "It might become a sublime epitaph.") I was sure Haili was not interested in the immortal honor and just had her eye on the prize money. For heaven's sake, how could those Jersey guys expect the Nobel Committee to accept their nomination? The plot hatched from Haili's novel was getting more farcical by the hour.

I went to Kaiming's office to discuss the story with him. He had been writing an article on U.S. weapon sales to Taiwan and, at the sight of me, turned away from his computer. I told him I feared that things were getting worse. But he viewed the new developments differently—he believed, in fact, that the frauds were on edge now, perhaps feverish and trembling with fear. But they couldn't simply slam the brakes on wheels that they had already set in motion—they had to play off their nerves as nonchalance. Otherwise, they'd lose face publicly and get hammered by their enemies. Gu Bing could even be removed from his office if he admitted any misconduct. "They're riding a tiger and can't get off," Kaiming concluded and screwed up an eye. He was always sure of his views.

He'd just had his hair cut and looked younger today—his head seemed rounder than usual and his jaw smoother. He held his sinewy hand over his steaming teacup, which reminded me of his hobby of sailing alone on the ocean as a way to clear his mind. He emphasized, "We must continue to expose their lies."

I realized that Kaiming had also been following the case closely. Despite his cordial relationship with the Chinese authorities, he always wanted to remain neutral in our news reporting so that we could grow our reputation as an unbiased source for Chinese readers around the world—a source that reported all the news Xinhua wouldn't. Indeed, people had begun to view GNA that way, and every month our readership increased by thousands. Lately Kaiming had also been expanding his small publishing house, which brought out books on people and issues and historic events that could not be discussed openly in China. His books were selling well in Hong Kong and at some airports in Southeast Asia, mostly to the mainland Chinese traveling through. Secretly, Kaiming was even more ambitious than he seemed. He played his cards close to the chest. Only once, tipsy in a restaurant and together with two relatives, had he confessed that he saw himself as a sort of modern-day Joseph Pulitzer, and hoped to be remembered like the newspaper magnate. That was why he'd been planning to publish GNA's own newspaper and magazine all over the world once he had accumulated enough wherewithal. I admired him, needless to say. He had just turned forty-three and was already a self-made man, who had his own businesses, two beautiful children, and a loving wife. He was success personified.

Following my boss's instructions, I began to fact-check Haili's latest claims about her novel. The translator Edward Silverwood, famous in China thanks to his several TV appearances there, was a professor of East Asian studies at Duke. I had phoned him in the morning, but he was not in his office. Around midafternoon I dialed again, and on the second ring a slightly rough-edged voice answered. It was Professor Silverwood, who had the voice of an old man though he wasn't yet fifty. He sounded like he had been working late the night before and hadn't gotten enough sleep. He seemed stumped when I mentioned Haili's novel.

"Remind me of the author again," Silverwood said.

"Yan Haili," I told him.

"Male or female?"

"A woman."

"Doesn't ring a bell. Did you read the novel?" His voice perked up.

"I went through six chapters."

"Is it a good book?"

"What can I say? It's below average."

"Then I'm glad I didn't touch it. I have so much to do at the moment that I can't take on anything new."

That made sense—I'd heard that there was always a long line of Chinese writers waiting for him to translate their works despite his high price: in addition to the translation fee paid by the publisher, the authors had to split their royalties with him, fifty-fifty. You may protest that's not fair, but it was his policy. What's cheap can never be first-rate. That's why some Chinese authors, especially those who were members of the Writers' Association and drew salaries from the state, simply let Silverwood have all the royalties from their English editions, considering that his translations could help them open doors to the other foreign book markets, and that European publishers often based their offers on the advance that Silverwood's English version had commanded.

Silverwood's process was to read a manuscript, write a short summary, translate the one or two chapters he deemed most interesting, then let his agent shop the translation proposal to publishers in New York. If the book was bought, he'd go ahead and finish it. But just two months back he had confessed to a Chinese audience in a TV interview that his desk drawers were packed with rejected proposals of that kind. He admitted that he simply had no eye for what could sell. To date, he had translated more than thirty titles, but not one of them had become a best seller. He couldn't even tell which one he liked most. Yet he hadn't lost heart. He held on to his dream of translating a landmark work like *Doctor Zhivago,* which, more than half a century after its first publication, still sold forty thousand copies a year in the United States alone.

Now, our phone conversation verified that there was no English translation of Haili's novel. This had wide implications—it meant that the translations into "more than thirty languages" her editor had bragged about didn't exist either. Many of them would have had to be based on the English version, because Chinese is such a difficult language that some countries have no translators who can read the original.

The next step was to contact Panorama Pictures in Hollywood. I called their office twice that afternoon, but no one answered. Not until the next day around noon did I get to speak with the manager of the studio. The man was as baffled by my questions as Silverwood had been.

"Come again," he said.

"Love and Death in September," I repeated.

"Never heard of it. You sure it's our company that bought it?"

"Yes, Panorama Pictures."

"Well, you can't take that kind of rumor seriously. If a script sold for more than a million dollars, the whole of Hollywood would have heard of it. Do you know who her agent is?"

"I've no clue."

"This sounds bogus." He giggled childishly. "One thing I can tell you—we haven't acquired any script recently."

I thanked him and hung up. I couldn't help but feel happy that Haili's house of cards was starting to tumble. I debated whether to confront her again with the lies I had just ferreted out. Should I inform my boss of my new discoveries and get them published right away? Or should I give Haili a chance to make amends?

I telephoned her at the prep school where she was a music teacher and told her that I had questions for her, but she was busy in a parent-teacher conference and suggested we meet in person. Reluctantly, I agreed to see her at Lovely Songs in downtown Flushing the next evening.

SIX

To my surprise, Haili didn't show up at the bar alone. With her was a slight young woman dressed in a yellow raincoat and polka-dot boots. I recognized her at once—her name was Shao Niya. She was a staffer at NYU and also ran the website of a Chinese-language newspaper, *The North American Tribune,* which circulated mainly in New England. She was from Harbin and spoke Mandarin impeccably, like a radio broadcaster, as many people from that area did. Haili introduced Niya as her best friend, and the woman stretched out her tiny hand, which felt forceful when I shook it. The bar was noisy and crowded, packed with businesspeople, yuppies, and tourists, so we requested a quieter place to sit. A reedy girl wearing an orange apron led us into a small karaoke room. She turned up the lights a little and shut off the soft Hong Kong music when I asked.

After we sat down on the synthetic leather sofas, I ordered tea, fruit salad, and spiced peas and nuts for all of us. The moment the girl left, Haili said to me, "What's up?" Her eyes bored into me, her brows furrowed.

"I've discovered more about your salacious novel," I told her. I glanced at Niya, who had removed her raincoat to reveal a mauve silk shirtdress and was now looking around absentmindedly.

"What's up?" Haili repeated.

"Your brilliant novel, which you claim is being worked on

by the most famous translator in the industry? I called Edward Silverwood and he said he'd never heard of you."

"I didn't say he was my translator, did I? That was wrong information someone else gave, perhaps due to a misunderstanding. In fact, I'm doing the translation myself."

Her audacity astounded me—I knew that her written English was still puerile. True, she spoke the language with only a trace of an accent and could toss out expressions like "I'll be damned," "long time no see," and "twenty-twenty hindsight," but every once in a while she still made mistakes, calling out "break your leg" instead of "break a leg," or urging someone to "crack your brain" in place of "rack your brains." She used to tell others that sweepstakes had "cheated on" her, because she had paid a $19.95 fee twice but never been able to collect the big prizes they'd promised her. Exasperated once, she had declared "I'm mad about Cicely," Larry's youngest sister, who had ignored her advice and dropped out of college to join a local band.

In fairness, Haili had always been above the kinds of silly mistakes made by her former schoolmates. She'd told me that one of them, while filling out a visa application form at the U.S. consulate in Shenyang, had even put down "twice a week" on the line for "Sex." But it would take years for Haili to be able to produce publishable English prose. What she was capable of now was bubbly and ridden with clichés.

The waitress stepped in and served the tea and snacks. With a toothpick I lifted a piece of pineapple, which tasted fresh and succulent. I said to Haili, "Truth be told, George Bush might not enjoy your translation."

"I've never said the White House was interested in my book. Don't play the wise old man again."

Before I could respond, Niya chimed in, "It was Gu Bing who announced the completion of the English translation and the possible endorsement from President Bush. Haili has nothing to do with those announcements."

I was struck that Niya was so well informed about the case. What's it to her? I wondered. Is she involved too? Is she playing Haili's publicist? Do we have a gang of four now?

"See, you made a false assumption about me again," Haili continued, pointing at my nose. "For good or ill, you and I shared the same roof and bed for two years, we ate from the same pot, and for more than three years we were a married couple. You should at least have treated me more decently."

"Hang on a second," I said. "I haven't finished yet. I spoke with the manager of Panorama Pictures as well. They'd never heard of your grand novel or any movie script based on it. Where did you get your fortune of 1.3 million dollars?"

Silence ensued. Haili was biting down on her lower lip as though she had too much to hold back.

Then she said, "I have written a script, and a movie company has been considering it."

"It must be a studio in Changchun or Kunming or Chengdu, right?" These were provincial capitals where some old-fashioned movie companies were based, mostly in dormancy.

"No, it's a U.S. filmmaker."

"Which one? Can you disclose its name to Niya and me?"

"I already know which one," Niya put in.

"We can't share the information with you," Haili said, "or you will rain on our picnic."

"That's a load of bull. If you cannot name the company, I'll have to take the movie deal as a pack of lies."

"Danlin," Niya resumed, "I can guarantee you that Haili is finishing a movie script. Your doubts are groundless."

"See, she hasn't even completed it yet, so how could it have been sold?"

"We've been negotiating," Haili said.

"Even if that's true, there's still no contract. Where did you get your 1.3 million dollars? This sounds like pure fantasy to me."

"We're almost there. I'm positive my script will bring a price like that. My publisher is experienced in closing this kind of deal. Everything will work out to our advantage."

"That's not very convincing, is it? I don't care about how big your fortune *will* be. I just want you to show the first page of your contract. How else can you prove your claims to the public?"

"The public is manipulated and misled by so-called journalists like you. The truth is, you can't let a day pass without using your job to tear other people down. Why, why are you so determined to humiliate me? How the hell will my success diminish you? I can't think of any reason except that you enjoy watching me suffer."

"Don't twist things around and accuse *me* of anything. Didn't you tell a flat-out lie in the first place? Haven't you been exploiting people's pain and loss with this novel?"

Haili shaded her face with her narrow palm and broke into sobs, wiping her prominent cheeks with her fingers and sniffling. "What have I done to deserve this?" she wailed.

Niya shot me a hard look and spat, "What kind of man are you? Don't you have a heart? Why do you take so much pleasure in tormenting her?"

"Honestly, I don't enjoy meeting either of you. I just want to stop this hoax before it spins completely out of control. If it keeps snowballing, some names will be ruined and many of us will get embarrassed. A lot of Chinese here will be ashamed."

"Then you ought to quit asking questions you don't like the answers to." Niya glowered at me, her large eyes smoldering.

"It's my job," I said. "I can't do otherwise."

"You just enjoy being a wet blanket."

"Who are you? You're a toady and a snob. As a reporter I cannot lie to the public."

Niya looked astonished, her eyes going to discs and her cheeks reddening. But she pressed on. "You're blowing everything out of proportion—this is overkill."

Haili sniveled and blubbered, "He always looks down on me and treats me like dirt. He's full of himself and is vendetta incarnate. He despises Chinese women and hates any of us who succeed, he's malicious like a mad dog, he's a snake coiling around my feet—"

"Goddamn it, stop acting the victim!" I cried. "Are you going to fall into a faint next?" I remembered the wrong she'd done me. Didn't she hand me the divorce papers the day after my arrival in America? Didn't she force me to share the legal cost of our divorce even though I hadn't yet found my first job here? Didn't she hide away her savings so the court could not award me a penny? Didn't she malign me, saying I was incapable in bed but still behaved like a male chauvinist pig? Didn't she lie in a personal essay that I had once given her a black eye in a bakery because she did not agree to buy two pounds of mung-bean cakes? Didn't she say that Chinese men were good only as bookkeepers, cooks, waiters, gardeners, caregivers, masseurs, and hooligans? The more those memories swirled in my head, the more furious I got. If Niya weren't there, I might have blown up. It was smart of Haili to have brought that woman along. I breathed in and out. I stood and picked up my umbrella. "Let's be rational about the position we are in," I told my ex-wife. "I can't gloss over all the fraudulence, nor can I lie on your behalf. You owe the public an explanation and an apology. Don't procrastinate—the longer you remain in denial, the more denunciations you'll face. Better scramble out of the hole you dug for yourself as soon as you can." I turned and headed out to the bar to settle the bill.

"Fuck you!" Haili yelled. "You only have the balls to bully a woman in distress."

Turning my head halfway back, I cried, "Yes, I'm a male groupie crazy about a celebrity like you. That's your price for fame."

"Let me alone, you jerk! I know you're a Taiwanese agent. Damn you!"

"Louder, louder, scream the house down if you can!" I flipped her off over my shoulder.

Some people, mostly from mainland China, called me a Tai-wanese agent, believing that I was paid to write in support of Taiwan's interests. But that accusation was groundless; I wrote only of my own volition. True, a businessman based in Taipei but acting as an official agent here had once approached me with a check for eighty thousand dollars and asked me to publish an article in defense of the Taiwanese government's policies every month, but I declined the offer. I've heard that some exiled Chi-nese writers in North America do accept that kind of money, but I would never do that. I wanted to remain independent.

SEVEN

I filed my second column on the scandal. In it, I quoted from the original press release announcing that *Love and Death in September* was being translated into thirty languages and threw that claim against my own conversation with Silverwood, where he had denied even having heard of the novel. "Yan Haili is calling this a misunderstanding and now claims to be doing the translation herself," I wrote. "How many different stories will she fabricate before she finally admits the truth?" I also mentioned that the Nobel Prize Nomination Committee in New Jersey was busy composing their Nobel nomination letter to be sent certified to Stockholm—the letter wasn't difficult to write, I noted drily, but they couldn't yet find a person among them capable of rendering it into formal English. I threw in the movie deal as well. "Jiao Fanping claimed that Panorama Pictures in Hollywood had just purchased the script adapted from the novel for 1.3 million," I wrote, but I did not elaborate, willing to leave Haili a little room to salvage her reputation. Everyone could still see that this was the latest installment in their ongoing charade.

My boss liked my piece, though he mused with a grin, "You didn't put enough of your usual fire into it, Danlin. You shouldn't let your personal relationship with that heartless woman hold you back. The power of your pen comes from your lack of reverence for propriety and relations. Don't lose your nerve."

I said, "Let's hope this will bring the whole thing to a conclusion."

"It might not be so easy."

The column was posted and began circulating with a vengeance. More uproar broke out, ranging from condemnation to ridicule. Some people called Haili "a cheap whore" and those involved in the scheme "scumbags of China" and "human dregs." People were greedy. The moment a huge sum of money was mentioned, they got fired up. Inevitably, a raft of trolls began to emerge, all posting under noms de web, all attempting to outdo one another with more and more outrageous comments. Most of them seemed to be women who had a lot of free time on their hands and took pleasure in another woman's downfall (though some disguised themselves as men). One claimed that she had known Haili for more than a decade and never believed a word of what she said. "With her around, you always feel as if there is a time bomb ticking close by," she wrote. "Worse, when Yan Haili and I were roommates in Shanghai, she told others that she had been born and raised in Beijing. In truth, her mother had given birth to her on a straw mat in some hick town in Liaoning province." That was a far cry from anything you can call plausible. I knew for a fact that Haili had never lived in overcrowded, smog-swathed Shanghai. She was born in Changchun, which, though not a metropolis, had been the capital of Manchukuo during the Japanese occupation. Another commenter, who I was pretty sure was also a woman, declared that Haili was childless and could afford to be promiscuous because she had had a hysterectomy many years before. She wrote, "Yan Haili is not a woman anymore and has to take hormones every day. What a dead pussy!" That amounted to libel. I was certain that Haili's uterus was still intact. Someone else went so far as to claim that Haili had married an American billionaire, an oilman, who was older than her father. A few inquisitive ones volunteered to contact Random House and Panorama Pictures and then share online what they heard from those companies.

Yet two commenters raised the bizarre question of whether it had been wise and appropriate to expose this scandal right around the fourth anniversary of 9/11. If the scandal made the English-language media, wouldn't the story of Haili's shameless exploitation put all our compatriots to shame? Wouldn't some Chinese immigrants be singled out just like some Arabs in the United States who suffered abuse and intimidation (receiving hate-filled letters and bloody pigs' feet in the mail)? Wouldn't we be monitored by the FBI? We could draw brickbats to ourselves. So it would have been better to wait a while and, after all the commemorations of the tragedy had faded in the mainstream media, then bring up this case. "I am of the opinion that Feng Danlin could use more caution," one person wrote. Another chimed in, "We ought to avoid scandalizing too many people and keep this from lapsing into a feeding frenzy." Their misgivings irritated me. There are always worriers who'd give up eating, if they could, for fear of choking.

We dismissed their opinions as irrelevant, for in fact we wanted the English-language media, ideally some TV stations, to pick up the story. GNA had someone in charge of translating our stories into English—Wenna, a twig of a woman with thick eyebrows and a pointed chin, had written a summary of the case of Haili's novel and put it online—but, unfortunately, the U.S. media paid little attention to our reports. Wenna was an accurate translator, but she simply couldn't write like a professional journalist in English, even though she had earned a master's in journalism from Southern Illinois University and had lived in America for nearly twenty years. I knew how hard it was to write newspaper copy and to master the recalcitrant nuances of English, which the more you learn, the more slippery it gets. Deep down, I hoped that Haili would shut up about her stupid book, that Jiao Fanping would downscale his ambition to promoting it within China only, and that Gu Bing would give up on his plan for owning a German car and a modern apartment in Beijing. Although I believed that exposing Haili's scheme was the right thing to do, the last thing I wanted was for a Chinese author—even a hack like my ex-wife—to become an international joke, a perverse version of the American dream concocted by a bunch of crooks.

Three days later an article by Niya appeared in *The North American Tribune* and online. To her credit, unlike many others in the Chinese media, she always wrote under her real name. She said Haili was a debut author and unfamiliar with the business side of publishing. As a matter of course, Haili was ignorant of most of the details and arrangements that should not be her concern to begin with. Evidently her publisher loved her novel so much that he was beside himself with exuberance and couldn't wait to share it with readers. It was a fact that many translators were busy rendering the book into all the major foreign languages and that Haili had written a movie script based on the novel. As for the Nobel nomination, it was her fans' doing, beyond her control. She was more dazzled than anyone else—who in her right mind would object to such an honor?

Niya went on to say she knew that this author was a good, humble woman motivated by art, not ambition. In this, her first book, all Haili had done was let her pen follow her heart to verbalize her innermost feelings and thoughts, so readers should allow her time to grow—a novelist could master her art only by trial and error. Ultimately, Haili would be evaluated by her whole body of work, so no one should jump to conclusions too soon. Besides, there were many more urgent issues in the world, such as the invasion of Iraq—an imperial war waged in the name of democracy but actually in the interests of the rich and the powerful. And then there were the millions of Muslims being treated as dangerous militants, the Chinese government's suppression of resistance groups among the minorities in western China, the recent genocides in Africa, and the corporate scandals like Enron and WorldCom that had wiped out the lifetime savings of tens of thousands of people. "It was unconscionable, as well as remiss, for Feng Danlin to wield his pen like a sword over a weak woman's head," Niya moaned. "It will be better if he invests his time and energy in more consequential matters, engaging some bigwigs and fat cats and exposing them for sacrificing others' blood and lives for their personal gains. That will make Mr. Feng more like a responsible, fair-minded journalist."

I had not expected that Haili would use Niya to defend her so openly. This was a smart move in a way—to the casual reader, the article appeared objective and rational, absolving Haili of blame while placing more responsibility on her editor and publisher. I wasn't bothered that much by Niya's self-righteous rant, but there was an interview attached to the article, and it was in this brief conversation that Haili lashed out at me. She disclosed that Feng Danlin, the notorious essayist, was her ex-husband, and she insisted that pettiness was the only reason I was so determined to drag her name through the mud. She understood that our divorce had been hurtful to me, but I ought to have considered her feelings too. During our marriage, I'd been the worst kind of man a woman could inflict on herself, she stressed. She blamed me for spending more time with my friends than with her and claimed that I'd been such a wasteful spender that midway through the month we'd always be out of money. "He cared only about himself. He loved parties, bars, ball games. With him I felt lonely, miserable, and hopeless. How I yearned to escape, to get out of the disastrous marriage, but it was a long, long night that seemed to have no end. Naturally bit by bit the gap between us widened into a gulf, and finally we went our separate ways," she told Niya. In short, I was a selfish man "with a serious attitude problem." She then added that our "sexual incompatibility" was the primary reason for our divorce. "How could you satisfy your wife in just three or four minutes?" she asked Niya. "I'd wanted to love and be loved and to live a full, passionate life," Haili went on. "It's every woman's right to enjoy sex so as to stay beautiful."

I was galled by the personal attack, with which she must have intended to evoke sympathy from women readers while humiliating and cowing me into silence. It would feel so good to strike back. I thought about revealing how she had started an affair with Larry Clements and was even living with him long before I came to the States; how on my arrival in New York, she had lied about having found me a job in a restaurant so as to dump me at a seedy inn in Chinatown; how she had presented me with a full folder of divorce papers the following day. But I couldn't say any of that in a factual article about her novel. I considered writing something just as her ex-husband, a personal essay of sorts, yet I didn't know how to emotionally separate it from my reporting on the scandal. There was no way to make such a piece entirely detached from the case at hand. To tell the truth, I feared that if I revealed too much of how she had mistreated me, some readers might view me as laughably weak.

Maybe I shouldn't write such a personal essay at all. When fighting with a pig, you'll have to roll in mud. I would not debase myself that way. Perhaps just a brief statement would serve the purpose. I wrote:

Indeed, I used to be very gregarious and spend four or five evenings a week in restaurants, teahouses, and karaoke bars. But that was back in China, where without a network of friends, you could not survive. I allow that even though I was Yan Haili's husband in those days, I was still a young boy at heart, rough around the edges. But compared to most men around me, I wasn't that bad. I never betrayed my wife, never broke a promise, never gambled, never went on a bender, never smoked or splurged, and I was always willing to change—to become a better man. At home I let Yan Haili wear the pants, aside from the matter of money; that was because she would slip our hard-earned cash into her parents' hands. You all know it takes many years for a boy to grow into a man, so it is unreasonable to assume that the groom must know a whole lot about life and must be much more experienced than his bride when they marry. Men are human beings too and need time and room to grow. It was true that I was not a considerate husband to Yan Haili in the beginning and even ducked the role of our small household's mainstay. But gradually I grew into a different man, and now I even can enjoy being alone. I do not live beyond my means anymore, because I have learned how hard it is to make a dollar. Anybody who knows me can tell you that I am not cavalier about money, though I am not a tightwad either. Admittedly, I often take a critical attitude, but it has never bothered me, because I cannot abide a person devoid of their own thoughts and opinions. Without an attitude, how am I different from a robot? To be honest, I aspire to become a man with a forceful character full of strong opinions—in other words, a variant instead of a solid model. I won't mind being singled out as a party pooper. As for my sexual problem that Yan Haili referred to, it was an entirely different issue. Before knowing my current girlfriend, sometimes I did have difficulties with women like my ex-wife, who simply turned me off and made me feel not only henpecked but also emasculated. I couldn't bring myself to kiss her on the mouth, as though she were ill, her body fluids contagious (including her tears). Now I am proud to say that I am all right between the sheets. You may ask my girlfriend, Katie Torney, a professor of sociology at NYU, how I do in bed if you are not convinced.

I showed the piece to my colleague Lucheng, who was the man at GNA who approved my columns for publication. He shook his head and said, "This is too much. Boy, you must have been rattled by Haili's attack. This essay lacks focus and just rambles on and on. Besides, you shouldn't be so forthcoming about your private life."

"How else should I counter a personal attack?" I asked Lucheng, a lanky man with close-set eyes and a thatch of bushy hair graying at the temples. He held some shares of GNA, amounting to approximately six percent of the company. I thought about bringing up my writing credo, "honesty is strength," but I thought better of it. (My experience has taught me that if you mince words, or skirt an issue, or grab at truth only halfway, then you will stifle your own voice, which can't help but sound hesitant and weak. Vague language reflects a feeble mind or fearful spirit, so any equivocating must be cast out.)

"This is too personal," Lucheng explained. "You make yourself more vulnerable by exposing the details of your life in this way. If we posted this piece as it is, it would throw off your reporting of the scandal, and might play right into their hands."

"So I should just let this affront go?"

"You should first figure out who is behind Yan Haili. She must have strong supporters, otherwise she would've backed down long ago." Lucheng twirled a sharp pencil between his thumb and forefinger.

"It could take ages to find that out. Meanwhile, Haili is slinging mud at me in public."

"Still, your account of your private life will put you on the defensive. You must never appear apologetic in a situation like this. You're combating a brazen liar."

I thought about that and realized that my column could be somewhat feckless. Indeed, it revealed more of myself than of Haili. Also, I realized I ought to speak with Katie before mentioning her name in my column, so I told Lucheng I appreciated his opinion and would come up with something else.

EIGHT

I broached the matter with Katie when I went to see her that weekend. She said, "I won't mind if you mention my name. I'll tell them you're a hoot." She gave a short laugh, narrowing her green eyes.

"But don't make me out to be a weirdo, okay?" I said, suddenly anxious.

"Of course I won't."

"I'm not comfortable making this too personal. It could spiral into other areas of our lives." I said that also as a reminder for myself to be more professional, not to write like an essayist when I was doing journalism.

"You have a point there," Katie said.

After dinner she went to her bedroom to grade papers while I put on my denim overalls and resumed work on the built-in bookcase I'd been making for her. It was constructed of plywood and poplar wood, four feet high along a wall in her study. I had already assembled all the pieces and now needed to sand it down. After that, I would install the crown molding and paint the whole thing white to match the wall. As I started rubbing the wood with sandpaper, music throbbed from Katie's room. She was listening to a punk rock band. Katie's father had been an engineer in the air force. Except for three years in Okinawa in the early 1980s, she had grown up in Georgia and South Carolina. I often teased her, saying she ought to have taken to country or gospel instead of punk music. I did not enjoy that type of music. My love was classical music—Bach, Tchaikovsky, Mendelssohn, and especially Brahms's symphonies, whose beautiful lyricism blended with a measure of pathos would grip my heart every time I listened to them. Whenever I teased Katie about her music, she would tease me right back, calling me a "fake aristocrat." In fact, I was also fond of some American folk songs, such as "The Big Rock Candy Mountain" and "Pretty Boy Floyd." Their melodies didn't impress me much, but I liked the lyrics, which expressed the sentiments of the underprivileged.

For the first round of sanding I used 60-grit sandpaper; later, I would switch to 150-grit. I wasn't an expert at carpentry, but I could make some basic types of furniture and could use all the hand tools (though I was still unfamiliar with some American power tools). I had learned the skill from my father, who'd been a master carpenter and proud of his way of living, which, even in the famine years and through all the political storms, had been "better than a doctor's," as he often bragged. The life he prided himself on was a materially secure one, offering him enough to eat and drink. All kinds of customers—young couples about to marry, newly promoted officials, and people who had finally gotten their own housing—would come with gifts and ask my father to furnish their homes. He never spent a penny on the wine and liquor he drank at dinner every night. Yet I wasn't crazy about my father's craft and didn't care about the creature comforts he relished.

My mother in secret urged me to read more books and study hard so that I could go to college, but my father made me learn carpentry, saying, "With this single skill you'll be able to make a living anywhere." I knew he meant to equip me with a meal ticket, but my heart was elsewhere. He enticed me by allowing me to keep all the profits from the sales of the small pieces of furniture I made: chairs, side tables, nightstands, cupboards. For a teenager, those profits were a lot of money. I spent most of it on picture-story books (simplified classics and revolutionary novels for children) and cassette and video tapes, as well as on snacks shared with my pals—rock sugar, peanut brittle, spiced peas, candied dates, dried persimmons. In our neighborhood I was known as an openhanded boy, if not a spendthrift.

Just last week I'd heard from my parents, and again they had urged me to have children with Haili. "She is already thirty-four," they wrote. "How long do you want to wait? Women older than thirty-six can give birth to retarded babies. You two must not procrastinate anymore. Please tell Haili to stop wasting the excellent genes you both have! Also, she should eat plenty of seaweed from now on to get enough iodine for pregnancy." I had still not told my parents about our divorce, the knowledge of which would have devastated them. They adored my ex-wife and often said she was far more capable than me and I ought to count my lucky stars for having married her. In their eyes she was still a model daughter-in-law. My sister and I had agreed to keep the truth from our parents, who these days were addled with age. They couldn't possibly imagine that their beloved daughter-in-law had turned into a different person. They still dreamed of a brood of grandchildren, and thus a lusty blood-line, from my vanished union with Haili.

THE NEXT MORNING I went into work and wrote my third column on the case of Haili's novel. I first responded indirectly to Niya's article, stating that I was entirely aware of the nature of the Iraq War, the purpose of which was mainly to secure the oil supply for the United States, so I'd been against the conflict from the beginning. No country had infinite resources, and the war would surely run up more debts, for which every one of us might have to pay more taxes. It cost thirty-five dollars to prepare a single hamburger in the U.S. Army deployed in Iraq. Imagine all the other expenses. As for my private life, it should be left out of this discussion, and all I wanted to say was that now I had a girlfriend named Katie Torney and that our sex life had been wonderful and wholesome. From there I proceeded to discuss the novel. I said that I stood by everything I'd written, and I had irrefutable evidence to back up my words. I ended by challenging Haili: "If you haven't lied to the public, show us the first pages of both the movie contract and the book contracts signed with the foreign publishers. That will stop all the speculation and send us to the bookstore to buy your novel, and I will gladly drink to your smashing success." I didn't mention Niya and meant to exclude her, because to my mind she was a bit of a freak. I couldn't help but wonder if she'd been betrayed or abused by men in her past. She might be a man-hater I'd better shun.

At noon Kaiming, Lucheng, and I lunched at a nearby eatery. The place, Chef Choi's House, was owned by a middle-aged Korean couple and offered mainly Chinese food. For five or six dollars you could have a full meal—fried rice or lo mein, plus a bowl of soup and a pair of egg rolls or chicken wings or a crab rangoon. I often wondered how they could make money selling the food so cheaply. I'd once spoken with the couple, who were from Gwangju. They started their day before nine a.m. and closed up after eleven at night; they worked seven days a week and took a day off only on Christmas. The spry woman told me, "We have two grandkids born here and our youngest son is in the U.S. Navy, so like it or not, here's home." She had Band-Aids on her fingers; her husband wore a back brace as he cooked. His backache made his shoulders droop when he walked. After that conversation, I couldn't stop thinking how so many people bragged about getting rich in the restaurant business, while so few let on about the amount of sweat and misery in the work compared with the meager profit.

Lucheng had once served as a junior propaganda officer in the People's Liberation Army. After he was demobilized, he edited a small magazine of international economics in Guangzhou. He had come to the States eleven years before, and though a workaholic, he didn't know English and only stayed at GNA editing the news gathered and drafted by others. When Kaiming went out of town, which he often did, Lucheng would run our company in his stead. In some ways he was our second boss— "Kaiming's understudy," in his own words. I liked Lucheng but felt he was too cautious and kept to himself a lot. His mind-set belonged to my parents' generation, though he was only eight years older than me. He had seen my third column about the scandal and didn't like it but had allowed it to be published anyway. "You shouldn't have mentioned your sex life," he told me, biting into an egg roll.

Kaiming agreed. "You might cause trouble for Katie, to be honest."

I knew I had been vain to mention my girlfriend's name to show she was American. But I'd also thought that might stop Haili from spreading the slander that I was a failure when it came to relationships with women. Now my superiors' words made me uneasy. "I was angry," I said, "but perhaps I should've been more restrained. But Kaiming, what kind of trouble could this cause for Katie?"

"Hard to say." My boss shook his head. "Just two days ago I spoke to someone at the consulate about Katie's visa situation, and your column connects her with you. That might do her a disservice."

Indeed, I had an uneasy relationship with the officials, but the New York Chinese community was so connected that they must already have known about Katie and me. Men like Kaiming and Lucheng had a sixth sense for politics, developed and honed in the revolutionary upheavals and political shifts in our native land, though they couldn't always articulate their thoughts and suspicions. I regretted having mentioned Katie in the column. "I should've been more cautious," I said.

"No use in worrying about it now," Kaiming told me, chewing on a hot wing. "I have good news. I just heard from Shanghai that *The Readers' Guide Weekly* is going to reprint one of your columns tomorrow."

"Which one?" I asked in surprise.

"The first one on your ex-wife's wannabe blockbuster."

"Men, this will make the scam known all over China," Lucheng said and burped. Indeed, the *Weekly* circulated nationwide and was attached to the Party's newspaper *The Guangming Daily*.

Kaiming went on, "This will also do us good—they'll credit us as the source. Congratulations, Danlin!" He raised his soup cup while Lucheng and I lifted ours. We touched cups.

Even as we toasted, I was a little flummoxed—official newspapers and magazines in China had rarely printed anything GNA published. They especially avoided my work because I was known as a troublemaker who wouldn't hesitate to embarrass celebrities and bureaucrats. There must have been people in China's media who disliked the hype surrounding Haili's book as much as we did, and wanted to cool it down. Yet it was too early for us to truly celebrate. In spite of my misgivings, though, I hoped the reprint in that weekly might put an end to the scandal.

After our lunch, I headed toward a construction site on Crufts Street to look at the apartment buildings in the making, while Kaiming and Lucheng, puffing on Marlboros, began to walk leisurely back to our office. They liked to play a round of chess before the noon break was over. My boss's right foot kicked a little every few steps, and Lucheng waddled a bit on his short legs. They both wore moccasins, Kaiming's dark brown and Lucheng's beige. Their relaxed gaits showed they were happy, at ease with their work. I watched them for a while. Oddly, I was moved by the sight of the two receding men, which made me see that happiness could be so simple and so transparent. This realization warmed my heart and, believe it or not, brought me close to tears. Underneath I'm a softie, something of a poet by disposition.

Ever since coming to America, I'd been fascinated by how homes were built here. Whenever I had a chance, I'd go into houses or buildings under construction, observing the insides—the vacant basements, the exposed frames, the scattered ceramic tiles, the dusty carpets, the fillings in the walls, the composite kitchen countertops, the fireplaces laden with craggy gas logs, the uninstalled bathtubs, the travertine floors in the bathrooms. At this site on Crufts Street, the three-story apartment buildings sat about two hundred feet away from the roadside and faced the sparkling bay. The last of the four buildings was still only a structure of pillars, beams, studs, braces, rafters, plywood boards, makeshift stairs at various entrances. Its top floor was being laid, and I could see all the box beams from underneath. I had visited many older homes under renovation and had seen solid wood beams, even steel ones, supporting the floors. Every once in a while a brick building boasted a slate roof. Now these box beams, together with the wires and plastic pipes exposed in places, gave me a feeling of shoddiness and deterioration, as though these apartment houses were not being built to last. I had once asked Randy, the supervisor of the construction team, why solid wood beams were not used. He said, "Matter of fact, box beams are lighter and stronger." That might be true. All the same, they gave an impression of cheapness and crude pragmatism that somehow let me down, like a devalued currency.

I had also asked Randy how much he paid his carpenters. "About twenty bucks an hour to start with," he told me. "It's not easy to find good carpenters and masons nowadays. Even experienced bricklayers are hard to come by."

"Twenty dollars is a good wage," I said. "I'm a decent carpenter, you know. I built my own bed." I thought for a moment. "Would you hire me if you ever had an opening?" I wanted to see if carpentry could be a meal ticket as my father had assured me.

Randy stared at me as if in disbelief, then said, "Why not, buddy, if you can do the work?"

The supervisor wasn't at the site now. A few workers were drinking coffee and pulling on cigarettes, seated in a patch of shade cast by a dump truck. They knew me, so nobody stopped me. The sight of the building's interior reminded me of my father, who had furnished so many homes, but our own home had always been shabby and even our dining table wobbly. This memory troubled me. I realized that my dad must have cared about his reputation as a master craftsman more than he did about his family's comfort. This made me see why I often fantasized about having a comfortable little house of my own.

NINE

My third column on the scandal, short as it was, provoked more outcries. Commenters echoed my challenge and demanded that Haili release her contracts with the movie studio and the foreign publishers. One declared that the IRS should be alerted to ensure that Haili could not evade taxes for all her new earnings—otherwise she might use the money for a boob or nose job. People must have envied her supposed good fortune—for $1.3 million to fall into her lap was beyond their wildest version of the American dream, although there were those in China who'd won lotteries with bigger windfalls and others who'd made much more from illegal business deals. There was also a sea of corrupt officials who had numerous ways of getting rich—kickbacks, hush money, commissions, free shares of stock, no-interest loans. Just last month it had been reported that a son of a retired top general had boasted that he would not consider any business proposal smaller than $5 million, and that he'd recently bought some eighty apartments in New York City as an investment. To protect their ill-gotten wealth, the Communist leaders maintained their hold on state power, suppressing whoever challenged their legitimacy. Despite growing popular demand, the Party dared not order its cadres to declare their personal assets publicly for fear of people's wrath. At the same time the Party, in the name of the country, had been amassing an enormous amount of cash for the day when it would have to buy international support to survive.

I had thought that Haili might retreat into silence for a while—at least take down her personal website, where her contact information was still listed. It looked as if she didn't give a damn about Internet outrage at all. She continued to update her site, regularly sharing positive reviews of her book that had just appeared in mainland China. She raised the stakes, granting Niya another interview for another Chinese-language newspaper in New York. In it she emphasized that she'd sold the movie script and that the contract was being drawn up. She said that once she had it in hand, she would release the first page publicly. As for her foreign book deals, people should contact her publisher in Beijing, who could provide the information on them—there were some business details she was not privy to or not in a position to divulge.

Niya asked her: "It's widely known that your biggest detractor is Feng Danlin, your ex-husband. Do you have something to say in answer to his criticism?"

Haili replied: "I have no words for that clown. All I can say is that I shall see him in court."

The last sentence unsettled me—was she really going to stoop to legal bullying? A colleague of mine had once been sued for libel, and because Chinese media companies didn't insure themselves against such things, she'd been forced to handle the case herself. It had dragged on for almost a year. She eventually won it but spent more than $70,000, only a third of which she got back from the plaintiff. She told me that the attorney fees were horrendous, more than $400 an hour. That shocked me, as I remembered that I had once moonlighted in a rug warehouse as a night watchman making $5.25 an hour. My colleague also said that although America was a land ruled by law, lawsuits were often a rich person's game—whoever could hire the most powerful lawyers would be likely to win. I feared that Larry might finance Haili's dragging me into court. If that happened, I would face tremendous difficulties. Like my colleague's former employer, GNA had no insurance against libel. Kaiming believed that we could handle any litigation by hiring an excellent attorney ad hoc. On average, one suit a year had been brought against GNA, but no plaintiff had ever won. As a result, Kaiming had developed a reputation as someone not to be messed with legally. He used to tell me not to worry about any litigation as long as I reported truth. Now I was unsure whether he would help me if Haili tried to take me to court. She might include GNA in the suit as well. A small part of me even blamed myself for engaging her in the first place. "A little self-doubt will do you some good," my father used to chide me. If only I'd taken heed of his wisdom.

For days panic had been eating away at me, and I couldn't stop brooding on what to do about Haili's threat of a suit. Had Larry been involved in the novel scam from the beginning? Did he also intend to make a fortune from his wife's book sales? Or was he behind the whole thing? Had he even been fazed by my uncovering the scandal?

I thought about contacting Larry directly to sound him out. Would that be too rash? I asked myself. But what was there to lose? If you don't get into a tiger's den, how can you catch its cubs? So I telephoned Larry at work, and to my relief, he agreed to meet at the Starbucks near his office building. I no longer hated him for wrecking my marriage, because in a way he had come out worse, being stuck with Haili. She must have appeared considerate and loving initially, but now that she had a green card, and was perhaps already naturalized, she didn't need to try to please him. It served him right to have such a devil riding his back.

In the café, he invited me to order some pastry. "Be my guest, pick something," he said, opening his leather billfold, which was shiny from use. I chose two pieces of macadamia biscotti, one for him and the other for myself. He paid for the biscuits and his coffee and my latte. The jazz was loud, a woman's hoarse voice scatting as if she were constipated, so we went to sit in a corner where it was quieter. Larry looked nervous and kept smiling, his face showing more wrinkles than it had when I'd run into him a month before. He blinked his lackluster eyes. I explained I'd been reporting a news story in my column that involved both Haili and him.

He looked astonished, exhaling heavily. "What's it about?" he asked and stopped midway through pouring Splenda out of a packet.

"About a novel Haili wrote." I pulled some pages of her manuscript out of my shoulder bag.

He stirred his coffee with a wooden stick. "I know she's been working on a book, but she hasn't told me what it's about."

"The main characters are a young couple—a Chinese woman and her American husband, who was tragically killed on 9/11. His name is Larry Clements."

"Really? You mean I'm in the book?" Larry looked oddly flattered.

"Yes," I said, "but you're supposed to have disappeared four years ago, lost in the rubble of the World Trade Center. Here's how Haili describes you when you first appear in the novel." I flipped to a page marked with a Post-it and began to read my translation aloud to him: "Larry was six foot one with long limbs, yellow hair, and melting blue eyes, and a youthful bounce in his step. When he spoke, I felt the air around me vibrating with his caressing, lulling voice. Though a businessman on Wall Street, he was also a philosopher, passionate about Spinoza, Kant, Hegel, Lao-tzu. Furthermore, he was highly knowledge-able about fine arts, butterflies and spiders, and European history. On our first date he talked in detail about how a nuclear power plant was constructed. I was deeply impressed and amazed. What a man! I kept saying to myself."

To my surprise, Larry giggled. "I wish I *were* like that. Honest to God, I don't even know how to build a table."

I was nonplussed but pressed on. "Okay, here's a passage describing your ass." I turned to another page and read again: "His backside, white like cream and perfect in size, dazzles me and makes my breathing flutter. I caress his skin, soft and smooth like silk, which reminds me of a baby's cheek. The marvelous feel turns me on, and I start showering kisses on his behind like mad, his skin wet with my tears. Oh, I'm so fortunate, so happy! I murmur in my heart and close my eyes." I paused for effect, then added, "That's quite a piece of ass, isn't it?"

Larry blushed. He gave me a lopsided grin and said, "To tell you the honest truth, my butt is hairy and perhaps smelly."

I laughed out loud, and he cackled too, one eyebrow tilting higher than the other. Our laughter drew the reproachful eyes of the half-Asian barista, barely out of her teens and wearing a bleached pageboy, a nose stud, and eye shadow that brought to mind a panda. I gave Larry an A for sportsmanship and said, "Tell me, to what degree have you been involved in this novel? Did you really not know anything about it?"

"I knew Haili was working on a book. That's about it. I suppose this is what anyone who's married to a writer always worries about—or hopes for: being a character in your wife's novel."

"It's intended to become a best seller in China."

"I have some idea about the Chinese book market. Over there you can sell lots of copies, but books are so cheap that you don't really get paid royalties. Even worse, there's no way to keep track of how many copies of a book they've actually sold. And every best seller has a couple of pirated editions there."

"Do you know Haili announced publicly that she sold a movie adaptation of her novel to Hollywood for 1.3 million dollars?"

"Jesus." Larry looked tempted to roll his eyes. "I wouldn't believe her if I were you. Sometimes her brain can get all worked up with wild fantasies and can't separate fiction and reality. She's an artist, very visionary, you know."

"But it's not a fantasy, it's a lie. The scandal has already been exposed in the Chinese media. I wish I didn't have to tell you this."

There was a long silence—even the jazz was gone.

Larry raised his head; his eyes flickered as though he was hurt. "Look, Danlin," he said, "I shouldn't go on gossiping about Haili like this. She can be nuts sometimes, and you shouldn't take her words at face value. She's too imaginative, all right?"

"I may not be taking her seriously, but others are. She has been giving interviews. She's amassed an Internet following of young girls who have already gone gaga over her. Her photos are all over the Chinese media."

Larry said, "Just keep in mind that I have nothing to do with the book. She's the writer, that's her business. I'm not involved."

"I'm glad to hear that, Larry." I felt relieved and thanked him for meeting me. If he wasn't involved, that also meant he wasn't backing whatever lawsuit Haili claimed to be filing against me. I wondered how he could be so cavalier about a scandalous novel that mentioned him by name, but like most Americans, he must not care about anything that happened outside his own country.

I TOOK THE SUBWAY back to Flushing. As I stepped onto Main Street, I remembered I needed a newly published memoir by a Zen Buddhist master in Taipei, so I went to the World

Journal Bookstore. Beyond the traffic held up by a prolonged stoplight, an advertisement for Continental Airlines flaunted a row of characters: WHEN WAS THE LAST TIME YOU HAD A TÊTE-À-TÊTE WITH YOUR OLD FRIEND? A giant Boeing, painted on the board, was forever sailing above those words, apparently toward the other shore of the Pacific. Another billboard admonished: ONE PERSON ADDICTED TO GAMBLING CAN RUIN A WHOLE FAMILY! A third commanded: SAY ALOHA TO ATM FEES! At the corner of Thirty-eighth Avenue a kebab stand was sending up little spirals of smoke, and the air was fragrant with the aroma of roasted meat. I stopped to buy a stick of grilled lamb.

"Two, right?" suggested the fiftyish woman behind the stand. She wore canvas oversleeves and smiled at me with a face like a dried apple. I often stopped at her stand; she was from Gansu province and knew me by sight; my usual order from her was two kebabs. I liked the exotic but genuine taste and the tender texture of her meats in spite of the strong seasoning she brushed on them over the charcoal fire.

I gave her a single and four quarters for the two sticks of lamb. Chewing the meat, I made my way up Thirty-eighth Avenue toward the bookstore. In front of a Cantonese restaurant I passed a straight-shouldered man leaning against a BMW and talking into his phone. "Fuck their ancestors!" he cried in Mandarin with a Fujian accent, his long chin jutted up. "Of course we won't let them. When you get there, rough them up some, but don't kill anyone." He hocked up a gob of phlegm and spat it on the curb. His bulging eyes glanced at a young woman and a little girl as they passed by.

His words almost stopped me in my tracks, but I continued walking, keeping him in the corner of my eye. I recognized him—he was from the Chinese consulate. I had seen him several times at public gatherings. He seemed too coarse to be a diplomat—he must have been a bureaucrat or the head of a guard unit. Why was he hiding in this side street, barking such frightening orders into his phone? Who was he speaking to? Why did he sound so exasperated?

The store didn't carry the book I needed, so I headed back to my apartment, strolling south along Main Street. The sidewalk bustled with pedestrians, mostly tourists and shoppers. At a storefront, a sign, planted in a pile of lychees, announced in Chinese: FRESH, JUST ARRIVED—$1.75 PER LB. There were also big pink peaches—four for a dollar, cherries at $1.49 a pound, golden husk melons at ninety-nine cents apiece, pitayas, pineapples, coconuts, longans, papayas, fresh dates, assorted beans, peanuts, mushrooms, walnuts, all at reasonable prices. I loved the groceries on this street—even their messiness gave me a feeling of energy and vitality. It reminded me of a regular county seat in China. The air smelled clean today, without the stench of rotten vegetables and fish, thanks to a thunder shower early in the morning. The sky was opening, islands of clouds floating across the blue, driven by a late September breeze.

Crossing Forty-first Avenue, I saw more than twenty Falun Gong, some of them in yellow tunics, standing before the public library, each holding a placard. HEAVEN WILL WIPE OUT THE COMMUNISTS! LET THE CHINESE PEOPLE HAVE OUR COUNTRY BACK! RENOUNCE YOUR PARTY MEMBERSHIP, NOW! NEVER TOO LATE TO REDEEM YOURSELF! CHOOSE YOUR FUTURE— HEAVEN OR HELL! In silence they waved the placards above their heads.

"They're so bold," I grunted under my breath. I didn't like Falun Gong much. They were zealous, uncompromising, mixing religion with politics, although in China many of them, classified as practitioners of a subversive cult, were victims of brutal suppression, crippled in torture chambers and trapped in prisons and labor camps. Haili's mother, a chatty old coot I'd never gotten along with, used to practice Falun Gong's breathing exercises every morning in Victory Park in downtown Changchun and would rage at anyone who raised doubts about her religious group. She even berated her bewildered husband for being an atheist without any spiritual life. Then one day she was summoned to the police station. Afterward she cut her ties to Falun Gong completely, never mentioned them again, and began to practice tai chi instead. She also warned her daughter, in her phone calls and emails, not to mix with the believers in the States.

As I crossed Kissena Boulevard, a black Land Rover pulled up to the library and released six beefy men, all Asian, all wearing work boots and dark sunglasses. They stormed the demonstrators and began throwing them to the stone steps. They seized the placards and stamped them to pieces; they wielded leather straps on the believers and struck them as they screamed. A woman shrieked as a thug beat her and pulled her hair. She was a nurse, still in her scrubs and sneakers.

The demonstrators cried out, but none of them fought back, taking the beating as meekly as though they had prepared for it, as though it had happened before. The passersby stopped to watch, and a few gasped. Some stepped closer to take a better look, but no one intervened. On impulse I walked up the steps to the attackers and, shaking with outrage and nerves, shouted, "Stop! Don't use force!"

"Go to hell!" yelled one of the thugs. But he stopped to look me over.

"Who sent you here?" I cried.

"Who the fuck are you?" another voice jumped in.

"Why are you doing this?" I shot back.

"Go ask your mother!" barked another man.

Before I could say anything more, all six of the men, as if on cue, withdrew into the SUV. After four slams of the doors, the Land Rover pulled away and merged into traffic.

"The Chinese consulate is behind them," a heavyset Falun Gong woman said quietly, wiping her bleeding nose with a wad of tissues.

A man with a black eye struggled to his feet and told me, "I recognized two of them. They've threatened us before."

My mind was awhirl. Now that the attack was over, I remembered that this wasn't my business—I felt uneasy listening to them. I wasn't Falun Gong, and their fight had little to do with me, so I walked back down the library steps, leaving the scene behind me.

As I turned the corner, I suddenly remembered the bulging-eyed man I had passed on Thirty-eighth Avenue. He'd been directing the attack from there. I felt a twinge in my stomach, and I turned around, hurrying back to the demonstrators to listen and write down their words. I also told them to call the police and report the incident, but they said they'd done that before and the cops couldn't help them. Nevertheless, the nurse dialed the police, saying they must update the record of violence committed against them.

TEN

I spoke to Kaiming about the attack in Flushing, and he was outraged. I admired him for his anger—there weren't many Chinese immigrants here whose hackles could still be raised like his. Just a few weeks ago a young woman had been assaulted on Maple Avenue in Flushing by a complete stranger, a man who'd slashed her face with a knife, but though many pedestrians heard her screaming for help in the dark, not a single person had intervened. They might have thought that the attacker was her husband or boyfriend. It was hard to persuade immigrants that domestic violence was unlawful assault, not a family's private matter. Kaiming told me to report on the Falun Gong incident, but not to antagonize the Chinese consulate overtly.

I reported the attack for GNA under a pen name, Elegant Brother, that I had used a number of times and grown attached to. In my account, I emphasized that only by chance had I run into the man who was directing the six thugs from a side street. As they'd attacked the demonstrators, I had tried to intervene and question them, but they'd only cursed at me. I wrote about this now not only to report the facts but also to condemn this kind of lawless intimidation. "We are in the United States," I concluded, "where any act like this will have legal consequences. The victims have already reported the attack to the police."

The article was posted and picked up by many Chinese-language websites and newspapers as part of their daily news aggregations. Though I'd used the pseudonym, I was startled to find that some people identified me as the author and even wrote me directly, posting their comments on my column. "We need more of this type of on-the-scene journalism, Feng Danlin," one reader wrote. "Let those hoodlums know they broke the law and will face charges." Messages like that disquieted me, because it showed my style of writing bore some signature that could not easily be disguised.

The Chinese consulate called us the next afternoon. I was in Kaiming's office when he took the call and let the official rant at him, insisting that we had distorted the facts and that no one on their staff had heard of the incident until it appeared in the news. My boss denied that he had known anything about the report prior to its publication. "Mr. Tao, we publish about a hundred pieces of news a day," he said calmly, "and I can't personally check every one of them before it's posted. But I can assure you that the writer of this article is not our employee. Elegant Brother is a pseudonym used by several of our freelancers."

Although it was Lucheng who approved pieces for publication, Kaiming as the boss could publish anything he wanted to. He had read my article before it was put out. Kaiming paused to listen. The caller, Vice Consul Tao, must have been demanding to know the author's name, for my boss said, "No, it's not by Feng Danlin at all. If it were, it would have appeared in his regular column—he's been too busy to write anything else. As I said, this writer happened to come upon the scene when the attack took place. Please read the article carefully—you can see that the author hardly expressed any personal opinion. He or she just recorded the incident and quoted the victims."

Seated in a swivel chair and chewing the inside of my bottom lip, I tried to guess what the caller was saying. Kaiming spoke again after a small chuckle. "How could we have known something like that would happen and dispatched a reporter beforehand? Like I said, the author of the article stumbled upon the scene by accident. . . . All right, I hear you, Mr. Tao. We'll be more careful and won't rush to publish anything like that again."

Hanging up, Kaiming heaved a sigh. "We might be in a pickle. Bastards, they'll never leave us alone."

I didn't know what to say and felt I'd done what I ought to do.

I GOT SOMEWHAT CARRIED AWAY and wrote my next column about my meeting with Larry. I reported that even Haili's husband couldn't trust her and had himself been completely unaware of her novel, even as he was depicted as the saintly husband within its pages. "In fact," I continued, "I had coffee with Larry Clements last Friday. He is congenial and unassuming, forty-something, five foot eight, his hair scattered with gray. He was dumbfounded when I told him about his wife's newfound literary stardom. Then he said I mustn't take her seriously. 'She can be nuts sometimes,' he told me. But everyone can see that this hoax of a novel was not due to absentmindedness. Yan Haili is a liar. Granted, she might have been inveigled into the scheme by her publisher, Jiao Fanping, and her editor, Gu Bing. It is time the three of them admitted their wrongdoing publicly; otherwise, we won't let them off the hook."

This article put new pressure on the threesome, but what shocked me was that Haili, without warning, turned up at my place the next evening. Katie happened to be there. I was unsettled to see my ex-wife's figure, double her normal size, through the peephole, but I braced myself and undid the door chain. As soon as Haili stepped in, Katie said to me, "I should leave."

"No, please stay," I urged, winking at her. I needed her to see and hear everything.

Haili glared at me but made no comment and just nodded at my girlfriend, so Katie stayed. She poured a cup of jasmine tea for our guest and placed a bowl of spiced fava beans beside the teacup. Haili glanced at the snack contemptuously. With a fistful of the beans, Katie retreated to the papasan chair near the window, about ten feet away from the two of us.

Haili appeared a little haggard; probably she'd been unable to sleep well lately. "You've become more and more petty. Why did you go to Larry behind my back?" she asked.

"Didn't you publicly threaten to take me to court? I had to do something. Honestly, I was shocked you'd kept Larry in the dark about your novel."

"So? That doesn't justify bringing him into this."

"Of course it does. What would you have me do? Kiss your ass and just sit tight waiting for annihilation?" I attempted a light tone but must have sounded quite desperate.

Katie tittered, then stopped short.

"I know you," Haili said. "You're vindictive and want to destroy my marriage."

I nearly burst out at her: Didn't you dump me like a bag of trash? Didn't you drive me to the brink of suicide? But I told her instead, "Your husband is wealthy. If he and you joined resources to bring a suit against me, I could lose everything. I'm scared shitless by just the thought of it."

"Now you know. Larry won't be involved. Actually, we just had a row. He's mad at me. It was you who lobbed a bomb into my marriage."

She sounded hurt, which softened me some. I said, "Larry seems to be a reasonable guy who won't give you a folder of divorce papers. That would cost him too much."

Haili smirked as if mocking herself. She glanced at Katie, who was leafing through my *Entertainment Weekly*. Haili looked hesitant, then resumed. "Larry's a shrewd man. Before our wedding, he convinced me to sign a prenuptial agreement. He always guards his secrets. I won't say he's cheap, but we have to split the household expenses."

I was a breath away from reminding her that when we had been together I would share my last steamed bun with her. Hadn't we eaten a bowl of lamb soup together outside the main entrance to my alma mater because we, two college students, didn't have enough money for two bowls to go with the wheaten cakes held in our hands? Though unable to afford a piano, didn't I buy her a keyboard? Was I ever stingy about anything she wanted? Didn't I promise to build a house of our own, a bungalow with a wraparound porch like the waterfront one in the postcard she had sent me from Vancouver? My eyes were welling up, and I averted my face. Haili had made this thorny bed of her own free will and ought to lie in it. It was no use for her to attempt to invoke my empathy—she couldn't make me cave anymore. A sadness mixed with a modicum of satisfaction stirred in my chest.

"Danlin," she continued, "I didn't come to quarrel with you. I came to beg you to stop meddling with my affairs, for your own benefit. You don't know what you've been up against."

"Is this another threat?" I asked.

"You can take it that way if you wish."

"Well then, cold or hot, sour or bitter, rare or well done—bring it on."

She smirked faintly. "You're still a dog that can never kick the habit of eating shit and garbage."

"You're right—I'm not going to give up."

"If you keep harassing us, we'll have to stop you."

"Who are 'we'?"

"The people involved in producing my book."

"You know what? If we were still in China, I might listen to you, but here I have to do my professional duty and report the truth."

"Truth depends on how you shape and present it."

"Let's say facts then. I've got to stick to facts."

"Don't give me that professional crap."

"You can't make me stop reporting."

"You're so naïve and stubborn. I guess that's why I liked you when we first met. You're still the same puppy at heart. The same young boy."

I wasn't sure whether that was a compliment or an insult. I said, "Yes, I was so naïve that I couldn't see how fickle and heartless you could be. If only I had known you would aspire to become a grand novelist as well as a big diplomat. Then I would've stayed away from you and—"

"Don't work yourself into a temper again!"

"If you apologize openly, even just one sentence, I'll get out of your way. It would be easy for you."

Her face clenched, twisted with annoyance. "Okay," she said, flinging up her hand, jade bangles rattling. "I've had enough of trying to talk to you. You can remain a truculent son of bitch and keep rocking our boat, but don't say I haven't warned you."

With that, she got to her feet and waved good-bye to Katie. Then to my surprise, Haili lifted her hand, her thumb raised and her index finger aimed at my forehead. "Bang!" she let out. "I'm not afraid of paparazzi."

Before I could respond, she made for the door. When the clicks of her footsteps had receded, Katie said, wide-eyed, "She's tough, isn't she?"

"She's crazy," I said. "God, how I hate her. My hatred for her makes me more human."

Katie laughed.

I stepped over to the window, and looking down, I saw Haili hurrying away toward Kissena Boulevard. She was wiping her face, then blew her nose into a tissue. Her shoulders were slightly hunched, shaking now and again. Perhaps she hadn't erased all her warm memories of me. My eyes grew hot, misting. Not wanting Katie to catch sight of my face, I turned and went into the bathroom.

ELEVEN

A few days later, on the morning commuter train to Long Island, I ran into Shao Niya. She was seated diagonally across the aisle from me. The train was only about a third full; at this hour, most people were going the opposite way, into the city. A gaggle of preschool children led by a young woman, all, including the teacher, wearing orange pullovers, were at the far end of the car, jabbering noisily. Niya's presence unnerved me a bit, and the thought occurred to me, unbidden, that she was shadowing me. Then I quashed the thought. She couldn't possibly be a detective or an agent, nor was I important enough to merit that kind of attention. I kept my gaze focused out the window. The trees along the railroad, oak and maple and beech, were just starting to shed their leaves, releasing them into the breeze a handful at a time. The yellowing grass billowed here and there, shimmering a little. In a gray-blue lake a flock of mallards was paddling, and among them a pair of swans cruised regally. Suddenly all the ducks took off, their wings flailing, while the swans, as if puzzled, sailed on in the ruffled water, propelled by canceled impetus. I wondered what had scattered the birds, perhaps a boat, or a dog in the reeds.

"Mind if I sit here?" Niya's voice startled me. She pointed at the seat opposite mine, blinking her round eyes.

"Not at all," I said.

She sat down, smiling and sipping from her tall cup of coffee. By its faint aroma I could tell it was French vanilla. She'd had her hair permed. The curls reminded me of a hen's fluffy rump, and she looked a bit frumpy in a hoodie and black capris, the edge of each cuff bearing a knot of twisted string like a miniature bow tie.

"What a surprise to see you here," I said. "What makes you come this way?"

"I'm going to see a friend in Port Washington."

"You seem to have friends everywhere."

"Is that illegal?"

"As long as you keep your nose out of my life, it's none of my business." I couldn't help but bring up this topic, provoked by the memory of her writings against me.

"Haili's my friend and I've got to help her," she said with a smile, showing a pair of thin lines bracketing her narrow nose.

"Has she hired you as her publicist?"

"Oh please. I've just been trying to give her a hand whenever I can, and I don't get paid a penny."

"It's very generous of you."

"I'm always generous to my friends. And Haili has been a good friend to me. When I came to New York and was broke and jobless, Haili was the only person willing to help. She took me in for a month."

"When was that?"

"Eight years ago. After I landed a job, I wanted to pay her back, but she wouldn't take money from me, so I bought her a yoga club membership."

"I didn't know she could be generous."

"Danlin, you were once her husband and you should have some sympathy for her."

"You don't know how she treated me."

"I heard she handed you the divorce papers the day after you arrived here. She was wrong, but that was long ago. You shouldn't be still angry at her, heaping wrong on wrong. That doesn't make it right."

"I'm not vindictive. I just try to report the truth. And you shouldn't be so involved."

"I hate to see my friend suffer."

"You can't save her. Find another opportunity to show her your gratitude. I won't let her get away this time, not until she drops her vanity and admits her fault publicly."

"I can see that you still have a lot of feelings for her."

"Only negative feelings."

"You rushed into the fray with so much passion that you cannot get out of it. You ought to be rational about this, Danlin. What's at stake here? It's just a romance novel—it's not worth the time you've been spending on it."

"My boss assigned this story to me, and with good reason. Haili and those behind her have been exploiting 9/11. They're profiting from people's pain and loss."

"Who hasn't made use of the tragedy? The White House has been using it, the Chinese government has been using it, Islamic militants have been using it, oil companies have been taking advantage of it, and every gas station has been benefiting from it. None of us can separate ourselves from the tragedy now that it has happened. We're all part of it."

"I don't know how to figure you out." I was amazed a friend of Haili's could speak so rationally. Then I realized she might just mean to absolve Haili, and her argument didn't sound convincing at all, but at the moment I had no idea how to refute it.

"I'm not as awful as you think. Take me simply as a woman who's never forgetful and always repays kindness and insults alike. By the way, I saw your girlfriend on campus the other day. She's attractive, a picture of fitness, but isn't she too big for you?"

The corner of Niya's mouth tilted a bit, giving her oval face a wry expression.

"You mean too tall? We're the same height, five foot ten. At least you can see that I can get along with a woman. Don't you think Katie is sexy?"

"The word *sexy* sounds ugly to me, equivalent to 'a good lay.'" Her eyes shone at me.

I laughed, tipping my head back. Over the PA, the conductor announced that Great Neck was approaching. I said to her, "I see your point. Just keep in mind that I don't treat women as sex objects, although I'm fond of them. So long."

As I was walking away, she waved with her coffee cup, but her face dimmed a little as though a shadowy thought had crossed her mind. She seemed quite reasonable, and I hoped she would stop acting like Haili's loaded gun.

I unlocked my bicycle parked at the train station and pedaled toward GNA.

FOR YOU, my colleague Wenna mouthed and handed me the phone. She simpered and licked her plump lower lip.

The caller introduced himself as Gu Bing and said he wanted to meet with me in person. He spoke casually, as if we'd met before and been familiar with each other. It took me a while to realize that the man, Haili's editor, was in New York at this moment.

"All right, where shall we meet?" I tried to remain calm even as my pulse was racing.

"I'm staying in the Chinese consulate," Gu said. "Can we meet here?"

"Well . . . that's kind of inconvenient." I paused, uneasy at the thought of stepping foot in that building. "How about meeting at the side entrance to Port Authority on Forty-second Street? From there we can go to a quiet place. The bus terminal isn't too far from the consulate, and there're some good bars and cafés in that area."

Gu and I agreed to meet there at two the next afternoon. Hanging up, I couldn't help fidgeting. Had that man flown all the way to New York to rescue Haili? Who was paying for his trip? With the kind of salary editors made in China, it was unlikely that Gu could afford the plane tickets on his own. He must have been quite desperate. The people involved in the scandal had started damage control.

Through my connections in town I found out that Gu Bing was here with a cultural delegation composed of nine artists and officials. This eased my mind some, because it meant he hadn't flown in just to deal with me. I talked with Katie about my appointment with Gu, and she also thought he might want to bring the scandal to a close. She had noticed that *The Epoch Times,* a Falun Gong newspaper, had just written about the case of Haili's novel as an example of moral deterioration among some immigrants from mainland China. The paper, free and available on every college campus in major American cities, also published an English edition and could easily spread the story into the mainstream media.

I arrived at Port Authority on time the next afternoon, a little wary about not being able to recognize Gu. I had seen photos online but wasn't sure they were current. It was warm for early October, the sky billowy with porous clouds and the sun dropping patches of light on the ground. Eighth Avenue was noisy and lined with yellow cabs, and the air was redolent of popcorn, cheese, onion, and hot dogs. Portly pigeons strutted around like little pedestrians, swaying their diarrhea-soiled asses. I turned onto Forty-second Street and, to my surprise, found Haili standing on the stone steps at the entrance next to a stalwart, broad-chested man. Gu had on a button-down plaid shirt with the sleeves rolled up, khaki pants, and two-tone saddle shoes. He looked like a golfer and was smoking a cigarillo, his free hand drumming on a thick brass banister. Haili wore spike heels, fishnet stockings, a saffron dress beneath a cardigan, and a pair of coral earrings; her face was lightly made up; a reddish leather purse decked with tassels and a brass key was hanging from her shoulder. I went up to them and shook hands with Gu Bing.

My ex-wife said blandly, "You two haven't met before, so I accompanied him to make the introduction."

"Would you like to join us for a drink?" I offered.

"No, thanks." She shook her head, then turned to Gu and patted the side of his wide jaw. "I'll see you at dinner, okay?" she said in a syrupy voice.

"Sure, have fun," he said.

She walked away, her earrings jangling, her bottom swaying. I couldn't tell what Gu had referred to—Haili might be on her way to a social occasion. The two of them seemed to know each other intimately. This thought irritated me, but on the other hand, Haili might have been purposely playing up their relationship to nettle me. I checked my woolgathering and took Gu to a bar beyond Eighth Avenue where I sometimes had meetings. He walked with an affected gait, his chest pushed out.

Gu ordered a whiskey on the rocks, and I had a beer. The young bartender, her eyes kohl-rimmed and her lips glossed ruby red, asked for my driver's license. "Do I look that young?" I said, my face burning. I produced my card. "See, I'm almost middle-aged."

"Thank you, sir." She nodded and began to pour our drinks.

"If she carded me, I'd be flattered," Gu said and gave a gasping laugh like a hyena. "You're practically a young man."

"If they raised the legal drinking age by fifteen years, I'd still be qualified. I just celebrated my thirty-sixth birthday. What an absurd law. I started to drink beer when I was a toddler."

"Where was that?"

"Changchun."

"Ah, I love those northern cities—the people are proud of the way they guzzle beer like irrigating fields."

When our drinks had been served, Gu said, "Danlin, there seems to be some misunderstanding between you and us. I hope we can sort out the confusion and come to an understanding."

I said, "I've spent a lot of time researching this story and know how you're involved. If Haili's novel were as good as you all claim, if all her accomplishments were real, there would be no news story here. But the book is a sham—you've done this to yourselves."

"I don't deny my involvement." He dipped his index finger into his whiskey and churned the ice cubes, then took a sip. "But I believe you're a smart man and understand we cannot let you continue your smear campaign. In southern China some newspapers have been reprinting your columns, and you're becoming quite a figure in a perverse way."

"Why would you find it perverse? I'm proud of my work."

"You want to make a name by ripping into others. For the time being you seem to be prospering, but believe me, in the long run no one can thrive this way. There're a few principles I've always stuck to, and they've helped me get where I am. One of them is never to attempt to gain anything by damaging others, not because I'm softhearted or solicitous but because they'll have their opportunities to get back at me—I don't want to make enemies. Young brother, be careful and watch the ground you're treading." He paused. "Let me put my cards on the table so you can reconsider what you've been doing."

"Okay." I poured the remainder of the Coors into my glass.

He continued, "In spite of your initial success as an essayist, you haven't published a book yet. I know that the Writers Publishing House is bringing out your first collection of essays, *The Raccoon I Cannot Chase Away*. What a title. I like it because it has a mysterious image in it."

"Thanks." I didn't know whether to be flattered or worried that he was aware of my book.

"I might be able to help you with the book. That's to say—"

"It has gone to the printer and no longer needs help."

He smiled as if amused. "Danlin, you're obviously new to the publishing business. You don't know that once a book is launched, that's just the beginning of its life—like a baby unable to walk yet, it needs a hand. This is where I can be at your service. I can help you promote the book in major cities and coastal provinces, and I can also organize at least two conferences for your book—events attended by officials in charge of cultural affairs and preeminent critics. Some of them will review it in newspapers and magazines. Next year I can nominate it for some literary prizes. On top of all this, I can see to it that the Writers Publishing House will take you on as a house author and bring out your future books. That means you can get a contract and an advance even before you finish a manuscript." He raised his eyebrows. "I will make you succeed in our homeland, not only because I have the pull and access but because I see that you have a great deal of talent. However, you and I both know that the world never lacks for talented people—everybody is a natural at something. What're scarce are the opportunities to develop and utilize one's talent and turn it into actual accomplishment. An individual cannot be worth more than others unless he has done more. By the same logic, if unrecognized and unrealized, talent is meaningless and not even worth having, because it will only make you more miserable and make you envy others' luck and achievements. Such negativity poisons your heart, ruins your personality, and transforms you into a misanthrope whose forte is only to upset life's harmony and deflate people's confidence. A talented individual without any accomplishment, at the end of his life, will be no different from an idiot." He lifted his glass and took a last, sharp gulp of whiskey.

I said, "Before I respond to your offer, can I ask you something?"

"Of course."

"When did you meet Haili?"

He looked astonished, then relaxed, a smile playing on his face, whose lumpiness made me see why a face could be called a "mug." "About three years ago in Beijing," he said. "She was introduced to me by a mutual friend who had just returned from Melbourne. You want to find out whether your ex and I began to fool around when you two were still married. Right?"

I nodded.

He went on, "I got to know her long after your divorce. She was introduced to me as a wealthy lady, the wife of a New York banker. To be honest, I was fascinated by her. What a lovely woman, sharp-witted and beautiful, vivacious, warm, outgoing, so different from some women who had just come into money and were greedy and unscrupulous. A woman like Haili can always make a man feel good and proud. That's why I started to collaborate with her on her projects. Now, enough of this. Tell me if you're willing to accept my offer."

I felt a rush of anger but lowered my voice to say, "This is

America, not China, where you can bulldoze small potatoes like me at will. Here people go by rules, and reporters publish the truth. You lied to the public, so you must admit your fault. That's the only way to stop my so-called smear campaign—by conducting yourself so that no one, not me, not the Chinese newspapers, can say anything negative about you. Once you've apologized, people will forgive. But I can't issue the apology for you. So to your fabulous package deal I have to say no."

Gu looked thoughtful. "I understand what you're saying, and if I were an American, I would apologize in a heartbeat so that I could put the whole thing behind me. But I have my career and life in China, and apologizing is not viewed in the same way there. If I repented publicly, my enemies would pounce and destroy me with the ammunition you've supplied. So I can't afford to admit any misconduct. It's the same with Jiao Fanping. We must protect our reputations and have no choice but to push ahead."

"But I too have to protect my reputation," I countered. "I can't allow you to influence my work."

"You're an obstinate man, Danlin. Bear in mind that you're not naturalized yet. You have a green card and some fire in you, but you're still under China's authority, and we can handle you as we see fit."

I considered telling him about my brand-new U.S. citizenship but resisted the impulse. If they'd known I was naturalized, they could have attacked me as an American, a foreigner who had ulterior motives against China. Instead I asked, "Then why did you come all the way to New York? Why meet with me, an obscure reporter, at such a place?"

"This isn't all about you. I came here mainly to see friends and to enjoy myself." He smirked almost in contempt. "You know, I was once a visiting scholar at Harvard's Yenching Institute. That was the happiest year in my life—I spent a lot of time in the libraries there. So I too love America, in my own way. I follow the NBA games, sometimes into the wee hours of the morning in Beijing. When Michael Jordan retired, I fell into a depression for months."

"Then enjoy the sightseeing and the ball games." I stood up, dropped a ten-dollar bill on the table, and stalked out of the bar.

TWELVE

My book was scheduled to be released in five weeks. Once it was out, Gu could have it panned by his critics. He had the power to cripple the book. The more I thought about it, the more agitated I became.

With Kaiming's approval, I went ahead and wrote my next column about my meeting with Gu as a follow-up to the pieces I'd done before. I quoted from our conversation, including his offer—his bribe—and my refusal. I commented: "This is how the literary apparatus in China works today. You must have connections and you must bribe those who review your books and bribe the officials and bribe the pseudoscholars who attend your book events. No wonder conferences are held nonstop in Beijing and other major cities to celebrate all the potboilers and propaganda pulp just published. I bet that for each appearance at a conference, a critic or cultural official receives a hefty bonus in a red envelope. Ordinary people like you and me, without pull or resources, have no chance of surviving in such a game."

My new column triggered a whirlwind online. Some people posted their comments directly on my column, and heated discussions continued on Literary City and other sites. Some participants must have been failed or would-be writers, probably many housewives among them who had a lot of time on their hands. They condemned Gu Bing and Chinese writers and critics at large, lumping them together as a corrupt group who lived off taxpayers, salaried by the state so that they could write full-time and party at will. (In fact, only hundreds of writers took salaries from China's Writers' Association now, and the majority, especially the young people, had to support themselves.) Still, angry commenters indiscriminately called the Chinese writers "parasites" and "idle elements of society." Some demanded that the Writers' Association be disbanded. Some asserted that Gu must be Haili's paramour and urged me to uncover their true relationship. "Who is this Yan Haili, anyway?" one asked. "A debut novelist nobody ever heard of. Why would that brazen editor in chief fly all the way to New York City to help her? She must be his bedmate as well as a business partner. Obviously both of them are barefaced con artists. Women from mainland China are getting increasingly shameless. Some of them don't think twice before selling their thighs, and some have simply become professional home wreckers." I could tell that this reader, who used traditional, complex characters rather than the simplified script developed by the Communists, must be from Taiwan or Hong Kong. Another remarked, "Beyond question Yan Haili is totally Americanized, obsessed with money and notoriety. I lived in New York during the attacks, and a neighbor of mine, an American woman, gave radio interviews, saying she had nearly been killed in the World Trade Center on 9/11 and escaped from the first collapsed tower just in time. But I saw her at home that day—she had a tiff with our building super, then went out for lunch with her former boyfriend. I can't see why people would lie about their involvement in the tragedy, as if it's glorious to be part of it." A third person wrote: "Most of you Chinese are just hypocrites whose words and deeds don't match. The whole world saw the girl at Peking University speaking against the U.S. to Bill Clinton's face when he delivered a speech on campus, but guess what she did later on? She married a white American man and is living outside Honolulu now. Recently she gave birth to a baby boy, an American citizen. Many Chinese women from the mainland are like that, two-faced, selfish, moneygrubbing, and opportunistic. Some are downright Communists or their fellow travelers." That sort of denunciation bothered me, because never had I intended to denounce Haili as an example of Chinese women who'd gone bad in America. She was just a petty crook.

I estimated, by the form of the characters, that there were more than a hundred messages from mainland China. This meant that people there had been following the case as well, and it would no longer be easy for the three to persist in their scheme. Many readers called on Haili and Gu Bing to make a clean breast publicly. One urged Gu to "finish himself" and step down from his position before being dismissed.

Both Haili and Gu remained silent in the face of the barrage, declining to respond to the questions raised by journalists. According to reporters, Haili wouldn't even answer the phone.

Contrary to my expectations, a few days later her publisher, Jiao Fanping, granted another interview to a widely read biweekly based in Shenzhen. He insisted that he'd been negotiating with many foreign publishers over the final terms of the contracts, but for now he wouldn't go into detail. "There's not a shadow of doubt in my mind," he stated, "that this book is becoming an international best seller. I am proud to have launched it and can't wait to share it with readers."

Jiao's nonchalance mystified me.

THE CHINESE CONSULATE rejected Katie's visa application again. She was crushed—she had planned a trip to China during the winter break. Without interviews from AIDS victims in Henan province, she wouldn't be able to substantiate a central part of her book. The consulate had told her that they were still assessing her attitude toward their country, which outraged Katie. She loved China, she insisted, or she wouldn't have spent so many years studying the medical conditions in its countryside.

I half-joked, "Maybe we should break up for a while so they can issue you a visa."

"You promised to go with me to Henan," she said.

"I'd be happy to if I could get a visa."

But we both knew that was unlikely now. Katie would still be able to get around without me; she spoke decent Mandarin and had connections with some faculty members at Henan University. We were seated on the sofa, and I put my arm around her and kissed the little mole below her temple.

"Don't worry too much," I said. "We'll figure out a way."

She leaned against me and closed her eyes. Her copper hair was shiny in the fluorescent light. "You know," she said, "last night I dreamed we had two kids."

"What were they like?" I got excited.

"Two girls, twins, both had big mouths like yours." She smiled, blinking her eyes.

"And they have large hands and feet like yours too," I said, fingering her earlobe.

We both laughed. Despite our laughter, I knew she was deeply ambivalent about starting a family. Her younger brother had Down syndrome, and she had seen how much sacrifice being a parent could entail. I felt her fear bordering on neurosis. Sometimes in the middle of the night she would press her face to my chest and murmur almost tearfully, "Don't leave me! Promise you will stay with me forever." But when she got up in the morning, she seemed to have no memory of what she'd said. I couldn't promise her anything, nor would I mention what she had babbled in her sleep. Once when she got tipsy, I tried to entice her to say those pathetic words again, but she only muttered, "You're just using me. I won't cater to your ego. When you've washed your hands of Haili completely, I'll tell you my true feelings." That stopped me from trying to get inside Katie's heart again.

In appearance, Katie was confident, calm, cheerful. It was sometimes hard to guess what she was thinking. She once confided to me that if her parents had sent her brother to a special-care place, their life would have been much better and they might not have talked about divorce, as they did every day. Lawyers, alimony, Social Security benefits, insurance. Yet even though they had grown "allergic to each other," they wouldn't file for divorce, because they both loved their son and were determined to look after him at home. Now the boy was almost twenty, thinking about girls all the time.

I was sure that Katie was fond of me. She might agree to marry me if I proposed, but I could not imagine a childless marriage. What was the point in living together for decades without raising a family? If I decided never to have children, I'd break my parents' hearts—and they might even disown me, so I was reluctant to consider marrying Katie. Eventually I might have kids, but doing so felt like an obligation—something I owed my parents. (My father used to harp at me, "You mustn't let our name die out.") Right now I was still fearful of married life. In the back of my mind often echoed the lyrics of a popular song: "Why do I have to continue my bloodline? / Why can't I live an easy life / And die alone at my own pace?"

Once in a while Katie would get a little jealous if I spoke with another woman on the phone for long. At the moment she felt insecure, uncertain whether she'd be able to live in New York permanently. She often said with a touch of self-mockery, "I might decamp any day." I doubted that would happen. She enjoyed the city's nightlife and went out to bars with her friends at least twice a week. I went with them one evening and was unnerved by the way she splurged on drinks, each of which cost more than the lunches I bought on workdays. I could hardly imagine her in a sleepy college town. She loved cities, in part because she had spent most of her childhood on military bases and had no true hometown. Perhaps only in a big city could she feel comfortable.

At any rate, she'd have to work hard for another year to get tenure, even if everything went well. Perhaps after that she would consider settling down. Despite her lovely, carefree appearance, the more I got to know her, the sadder her life seemed to me. Imagine, a pretty young woman had decided to close up her womb for good. It made me feel as if we were approaching the end of the human race.

MEANWHILE, something momentous happened to me. A popular news website in China, Harmonious Times, published a list of candidates for the one hundred top Chinese public intellectuals of 2005. My name was on the long list, surrounded by famous names. The nominations were a grass-roots effort by netizens, though the website had provided these guidelines: first, the nominees must be accomplished in their fields; second, they must have participated, in both words and deeds, in public affairs and thus have helped to advance social improvements; third, they must possess a critical spirit that embodies the principles of truth, justice, and equality. Although 159 names were on the nominees list and there'd be a vote by the public, my nomination surprised and overwhelmed me.

Among the nominees, I was the most obscure and was certainly one of the youngest. How could I be ranked among those economists, historians, jurists, environmentalists, sociologists, educators, passionate social activists, celebrated writers? Some of the nominees were exiled dissidents in North America and Europe, and some had served prison terms for speaking against the authorities. Four or five had recently died; one was buried in Manitoba, though a small cenotaph had been erected for him in his hometown in Hubei province by his siblings and friends.

My colleagues all congratulated me, and a few shook my hand, saying I'd surely get enough votes to be on the final list. "This is stupendous!" Lucheng said, rubbing his stubbly jaw with his palm. "Think about the odds—out of 1.3 billion Chinese, you got nominated. Amazing. You're already famous, Danlin."

"Must be a fluke, my good luck," I said modestly.

"Congratulations, Danlin." Kaiming clapped me on the shoulder. "Keep speaking out. The Chinese people are on our side."

I realized that my exposés must have reached a wider audience in our homeland than I'd thought. In recent years I had published a good number of columns on corrupt officials, celebrities, historic events, the victims of Tiananmen, the wives who would travel long distances to visit their imprisoned husbands who were political dissidents, and immigrants in North America. I had interviewed the Dalai Lama for *The Global Weekly,* a Chinese-language magazine published in New York, and later the piece went viral online. I'd been the first Chinese in forty years to interview the Tibetan leader, and my article made it clear that the Dalai Lama had never sought independence for Tibet—what he wanted was more tolerance for its religion and indigenous culture and more autonomy for its citizens. My interview ignited animated discussions among the Chinese, who'd been told from the time they were children that the Dalai Lama was a reactionary, a CIA puppet hostile to China.

I had also published a lengthy piece on the soaring real estate prices in Chinese cities. I pointed out that the continuous increase had been caused by the state's complete monopoly of land—the government sold the land to developers at exorbitant prices, which were eventually passed on to housing consumers (who were allowed to use the land for only seventy years). As a result, real estate had become the linchpin of the government's revenue, a hotbed of corruption and exploitation where investors, in collusion with officials, made profits. "Who has authorized the state to own all the land and to jack up the land price at will?" I asked. "And who is the state? Who has empowered it to fleece the common citizens? Confucius said: 'A rapacious government is more destructive than a preying tiger.' If we continue to let the state rip us off, we will be eaten up by this insatiable beast sooner or later. Who has raised this animal? Why do we have to feed it and let it grow into a monster? Are there ways we can tame and control it? I believe a state should be more like a guard dog than a preying tiger and must be obedient to its citizens." Again, that article prompted a vigorous debate, and people even argued about whether private ownership of land should be reinstated in China—this would be an effective way to curb the rampant corruption, some insisted, though I wasn't sure that could be the ultimate solution. If private ownership of land was to be allowed, there would have to be regulations to forestall speculation. Now, with this nomination, I could see that people had read my writings and given thought to them.

How grateful I felt to the marvelous Internet technology, which seemed like it would be China's deliverance and absolutely insuppressible. I kept singing of it to myself: with the Internet you can penetrate the barriers of censorship to reach tens of thousands of readers within hours; with it you no longer have to rely on the conventional means of communication monopolized by the state—you can raise noise and disseminate truth, making it known to the multitude terrified by power and expressing the thoughts many hold in their hearts but dare not articulate. It can give every individual a voice and every tyrant a shudder. It makes every computer a potential radio station.

All day I received notes of congratulation. One of them, to my surprise, was from Niya. She wrote: "Congrats on your nomination for a top public intellectual! See, it pays to make others squirm. I am impressed nonetheless."

I just replied, "Thanks."

I had no idea how to read her. She didn't seem stupid. Why would she become embroiled with *Love and Death in September*? However grateful to Haili she might be, she needn't follow her with such blind devotion. Did Niya despise me at heart? Did she write to mock and provoke me? Or to sound me out?

Katie said I should take the nomination seriously because it could lead to other things. As in academia, where a grant in hand could qualify you for more funding, Katie believed that my candidacy might open greater avenues in my career.

When I went to the Village to spend Sunday with her, she pulled two books from the bookcase I had just built her and handed them to me with a twinkle in her eye. "You should read these," she said. "They will help you understand your new role."

One of the books was a collection of essays by Noam Chomsky and the other a slim volume of lectures titled *Representations of the Intellectual*, by Edward Said. I knew the authors' names but hadn't read either of them. I flipped through one of the books and saw some marginalia in Katie's neat, loopy hand.

"Are they good?" I asked.

"They're great."

"Then I'll read them from cover to cover."

Usually I wouldn't finish a book if I found it tedious. I also had the habit of reading some books backward, one chapter at a time, as though first to find out how they ended, and to ascertain whether they'd be worth my effort. But I trusted Katie's opinion. I valued the way our relationship put me in contact with academia, a world of ideas, books, arts, and intellectual pursuits, which seemed extraordinary to me and beyond my reach. While it might be rife with politics, controversy, and strife, one could still exist more freely there.

THIRTEEN

By mid-October I had read the Said and the Chomsky. I liked their views and arguments but was somewhat underwhelmed by their writing. The authors' sense of the essay form seemed rather weak—most of the pieces were not carefully written stylistically, and some lacked shape and structure. In Said's case, this defect might be due to the fact that his essays had originally been a series of lectures delivered on the BBC, their lengths limited by the half-hour segment on the air. But both authors' thoughts and insights were rooted in their independent spirits and a constant engagement with the world. Their discussions of current issues often quickened and intensified their prose. Both were serious scholars, distinguished in their fields. Yet I doubted if either of them would have rejected an opportunity that could place them at the center of political power, say, overseeing a major ministry in the U.S. government. One can always march into the political arena under the banner of "get involved" and "make a difference." So many intellectuals passionately criticize power, typically when they are not political insiders, but once they become part of the structure, they talk and act differently, and even their personalities undergo a metamorphosis. Few have the integrity to stay above the temptation of power.

I know a number of Chinese in North America who became dissidents mainly because they had failed to land suitable positions in the Communist Party. Some of them still dream of becoming president of a major Chinese university, whose official rank is equal to a vice minister's. A few sick, old exiles, whenever I ran into them in New Jersey or Connecticut, griped that they didn't have free health care like the officials back home—they believed that China ought to have picked up their medical bills here. That was out of the question, so they felt disgusted with the United States, the richest country in the world, which forced its people to pay for their own medical insurance. One of them went so far as to claim that the United States had violated human rights, because the UN's Universal Declaration of Human Rights stipulates that everyone has the right to medical care.

Whenever I think of those men, my heart is full of pity and contempt. Many of them are like dazed travelers, jettisoned by the ship of politics but still fantasizing that they are on board with their former peers. They cannot put down roots anyplace, nor can they imagine life without a country or affiliation. They exist mainly in the past and in the clouds of memory. Their exile hasn't changed their psychology—they are still political animals.

I'm not positive that I could resist the temptation of a big offer from China. A consequential job usually comes with a high rank that guarantees a comfortable, secure life. Just work hard for a decade or so, make sure to follow the right superiors, and avoid stepping on any toes, and the Party will take care of you for the rest of your life. I have a distant uncle, a retired major general, a large barrel of a rustic man, who still receives his full salary. (In fact, he gets thirteen months' pay a year, because he joined the revolution during the Sino-Japanese War.) He also enjoys free milk and vegetables every day, complimentary theater and movie tickets, forty gallons of gasoline a month (his rank entitles him to use a chauffeur-driven Audi with tinted windows), a monthly periodicals stipend comparable to a menial worker's earnings, an allowance for a maid. His confidence in the Party remains unshakable. On my last visit to him, three years before, he had raved about the superiority of China's unique path, which combined one-party rule with a free-market economy. He even believed that China was becoming a model for other developing countries, an alternative to the Western democracy, which could easily fragment a sovereign nation. In his view, a third-world country simply could not afford democracy, which was like a strong medicine that not everyone could stomach. Look what had happened in Russia! Democracy would mean the end of the Party and the disintegration of the country. So we had to strive to blaze "the Chinese way." He was so convinced of this "Chinese path" that he'd have kicked me out of his home had I raised a word of objection.

That visit made me see how easily perks could trump principles. The Party is like the superintendent of a large warehouse, to which the common citizens are made to contribute parts of their incomes. Yet the superintendent alone has the right to decide who can have what from the warehouse. The privileged and the powerful enjoy the lion's share, while the rest of the citizens must shut up about the unfair distribution, because their role is simply to meet their obligations to the national treasury. All the cutthroat struggles and the lofty rhetoric about the necessity for authoritarian socialism (really a more brutal form of capitalism) boil down to this: everyone wants to secure the right to a bigger personal share from the warehouse. All the ranks and appointments are essentially certificates of different sizes of shares. Sometimes I cannot suppress a vision of the warehouse in flames. What will happen if it burns down or collapses or changes hands? This is the root of fear shared by all those who receive generous provisions from this warehouse, so they fight tooth and nail to maintain one-party rule and perpetuate the lie that the superintendent works diligently for all citizens.

If only I could sell my soul without a qualm! If only I could be happy with nothing more than fine food and wine. If only I were still an obedient child or a credulous fool. If only I specialized in official stratagems, smoother and more adaptable. If only I were a fearless statesman with nerves of steel, snugly wearing a flak vest of patriotism.

The truth is that when I was going through my naturalization ceremony, I knew I was relinquishing any chance of rising through China's officialdom to become a big man above tens of thousands of people and to glorify my ancestors. To be a free man also means to come to terms with my commonality, earning my bowl of rice with my own labor, taking responsibility for myself, body and soul, and accepting loss, uncertainty, solitude, grief as the human condition, as opposed to the slave's security and the caged contentment of a well-fed bird.

Katie also gave me a copy of *The Foucault Reader,* of which I read parts and then stopped. Though impressed by the philosopher's intelligence and incisive eloquence, I was puzzled by his writings. Perhaps I wasn't smart enough to perceive his intentions. Try as I might, I could find no enjoyment in his cynicism and his detachment from the world we live in.

PEOPLE OF CHINESE BACKGROUND like me have little sense of identity. In fact, the word *identity* is alien to us, and I still don't know precisely how to translate it into Chinese. I can approximate it by stringing together several terms, each covering a part of the English word, like *sameness* and *distinctiveness* and *status,* but there's no real equivalent. Its absence from our vocabulary might indicate a deficiency in our awareness of self, just as we don't have the word *bacon* because there's no such product in Chinese cuisine. (Another word Chinese doesn't have is *solitude*—as a result, we tend to confuse solitude with loneliness, an accursed condition often believed to be a Western malaise: "You'll end up a loner!" people will say. Or, "I love that great novel by García Márquez, *One Hundred Years of Loneliness.*") Growing up, we were all taught that we make our lives meaningful through serving the people and the country, that a good person must be selfless and think only of the larger group. In college I was assigned to major in journalism, and after graduation I worked at a state-owned newspaper. My role as a reporter was a given—I accepted it without question and even with gratitude. Most of my generation would have killed for a job like that. I tried to do good work and write well to carry out what my profession demanded of me. I made no real impact, though, since I had no say in what got printed. Like others, I had no will or voice of my own. I was more like a bolt or nut in a titanic machine.

My nomination as a public intellectual triggered an implosion in me, and I fell to thinking about my identity. A vista of possibilities suddenly opened in my mind's eye, and for the first time in my life I longed to become someone, to create an identity for myself to fit this nomination. I knew that people had nominated me not because I was learned and experienced, but because they wanted an honest voice that could articulate their feelings and opinions in the public discourse. A little guy like me must by chance have risen to the expectations of a frustrated, oppressed, silent multitude. I felt uncomfortable about becoming their spokesman, but I did want to be a voice others would listen to. Ideally I wanted to be independent of any group or cause and just speak from my heart, guided by my own sense of justice and decency. But how could I do that?

For days I'd been pondering these questions as I went about my life. Meanwhile, rumors about me began to circulate online, on social media, and in comment threads on *The North American Tribune,* as the inevitable backlash took hold. One claimed that I was a misogynist and that I'd once told a TV anchorman that Chinese women were materialistic and fetishized white men. Never had I appeared on TV or spoken to an anchorman. Another person insisted that I was a disciple of Ayn Rand, "the pseudophilosopher of the so-called objectivism," whose books I had never even read; all I knew about her was that she was an Americanized Russian émigré. A third person, a rumormonger through and through, asserted that I had always advocated the secession of Taiwan and Tibet from China. "As a traitor of our nation, Feng Danlin should be elected a public enemy, not a public intellectual," the person declared. "If he sets foot in China again, the government should slam him into jail or a madhouse." "Yes," another chimed in, "they'd best vaporize him like a fly." One woman even argued, "If I have the hots for a white guy or a black guy, it's my personal preference. Nobody has the right to interfere with my love life." It was my first taste of fame, which made me see that a public figure must endure public abuse and pressure, and understand why celebrities are often so passionate about their privacy—every blemish in their lives or personalities is magnified by the public while most of their virtues are ignored. Kaiming once told me that the biggest bore in the world is a proper celebrity, as if such a person by definition must have some character problem.

True, I had attended several meetings organized by the Tibetans and the Taiwanese living in New York, and on occasion I had stood up to speak my mind, but never had I said I supported any group that wanted to secede from China. I just told the audience, some of whom were mindlessly, rabidly patriotic, that we were not entitled to interfere with others' choices. If the Tibetans or the Taiwanese decided on independence, it was their choice, and we Chinese or Americans had better shut up about the ways others wanted to live. I also questioned the principle of so-called national unification, which is based on the assumption that the larger a country is, the more its citizens can benefit from it. "But what if a bigger country only makes people's life more miserable?" I asked. "Then how can such unification be justified? Why can't a country break up if smaller countries can improve people's lives? A large, multiethnic country's existence must be justified to its citizens, or else it will fall apart sooner or later. Without such justification, a bigger country can guarantee nothing but a larger national treasury, from which corrupt officials can steal more and the privileged can consume more." The Tibetans and the Taiwanese applauded my remarks and regarded me as their sympathizer. (Once a squat man stood up in the audience and declared in a booming voice, "I completely agree with Mr. Feng Danlin. So many of China's problems have in fact originated from the so-called national unification. The Chinese government always justifies its harsh one-child policy by insisting that the country can no longer sustain 1.3 billion people, so we have to control our population strictly, allowing every family to have no more than one child. But what if China were broken into several smaller countries? Surely that would solve the population problem. Think about Japan and Vietnam and Korea—they are all densely populated, but nobody in the world complains that those countries have too many people." Some angry attendees booed the man, but he weathered their scowls and deliberately remained on his feet for an extra few moments.) Of course, my liberal views tended to offend my compatriots, especially those from mainland China. At best, they considered me impractical and hotheaded. But unlike some dissidents, who believe in the use of force to topple a dictatorship, I balk at resorting to violence, which I dread might perpetuate bloodshed and destruction.

Many people responded to the rumors about me and expressed misgivings over my nomination as a top public intellectual. Some said I could be too radical or too controversial, considering my attitude toward China and women. Some believed I thought and acted like an American—too individualistic, self-centered, without any sense of ancestral memory. One even remarked, "Honestly, Feng Danlin often gets under my skin. His writing lacks sunlight. Why can't he write about some upbeat aspects of life? Why does an author have to upset and outrage people without end? He should relax a little and have a sense of humor."

"Sunlight on your ass, and I humor nobody but your mother," I snorted to myself.

I must admit that those people's blind acceptance of the rumors disturbed and hurt me more than the fabrications themselves, and made me feel as though I were facing a crazed rabble.

Now who can the rumormongers be? I wondered. My top suspect was Niya, because so much of the discussion about my candidacy had transpired on the site of *The North American Tribune*, which she managed. I took a deep breath and telephoned her, but she was not in her office, so I left a message.

That evening she called back. As soon as I heard her voice, I bristled and blurted out, "Why did you lie about me? When and where did I ever advocate the fragmentation of China? When and where did I say that Chinese women were masochistic, that they fetishized foreign men, turned moony-eyed in their presence, and enjoyed being sex slaves? When and where did I ever mock Chinese women as 'tofu burgers'? My mother and my sister are Chinese women, after all."

"Stop it, Danlin," Niya said. "I shouldn't have rushed into this mess in the first place. I didn't expect it would turn so ugly, so political."

"You haven't answered my questions."

"I didn't say anything like that about you. I helped Haili in the beginning only because I believed you were determined to wreck her marriage. You're still doing it, aren't you?"

"I'm just doing my job."

"To tell the truth, her marriage might be falling apart—she just moved out."

I paused. "She and Larry have separated?"

"I haven't talked to her about it yet, but that's what it looks like. Now you can celebrate."

"No, I'm not happy to hear that. Can you stop spreading rumors about me?"

"I told you—I'm not involved anymore. I don't want to get mixed up in politics. It's messy and ugly. You know I hate many of the Chinese government's policies. The moment I saw Haili and her partners using national politics to attack you, I called it quits. There are lines I'll never cross."

"So you're no longer against me?"

"I'm neutral from now on."

"How can I believe you?"

"All right, let me tell you this: you won't be able to stop the novel from becoming a best seller. The publisher has too much official support. His parents have infinite pull in Beijing. If I were you, I'd give up and let Haili go. What you've been doing won't heal your old wounds."

"All right, I hear you. Can you assure me that you won't meddle with this case anymore?"

"You have my word."

That pleased me. Taking heart, I offered to treat her to coffee or lunch that coming weekend. She tittered and said, "Don't bribe me. I won't do anything against Haili either—she's still my friend. But I wouldn't mind having a cup of coffee with you on Saturday morning."

"Fair enough," I said. I wanted to spend some time with her to find out more about my ex-wife's plans. Ideally, to work out a countermove.

Hanging up, I felt relieved. If Niya was no longer involved, I could focus on Haili and the two men behind her. I began drafting the next day's column—an article about the three degenerates, and how they'd been spreading lies about me with the intention of intimidating me into silence.

FOURTEEN

Haili published an article in *The North American Tribune* under the pen name Aurora Borealis. She called me "a megalomaniac and psychopath who is too big for his britches—a poseur whose personality defines malice." She added that I couldn't go a day without defaming others, that I had enough venom in me to poison a whole town, and that the only thing I knew how to do was tear down people who did better than I did. "It's understandable," Haili wrote. "We all relish seeing others fall, because someone else's spectacular failure can be a solace for our own mediocrity and ineptitude." (She could never kick her addiction to fancy words.) "He is a snitch whose long nose sticks out a mile ahead of his face. He is the kind of man who will do anything for five minutes of fame. If he wants to be famous for longer, he should throw his sorry self under a train after finishing a book. I am sure that some publisher out of pity would print it and use his death to promote it."

Then Haili mentioned a column I'd written about the recent arrest of a woman, "a snakehead" nicknamed Sister Liang, who had operated a smuggling ring in Chinatown to bring in illegal immigrants. Haili declared that someday I would be hauled in by the FBI or the Department of Homeland Security if I continued to interfere in the affairs of others. "Maybe a deportation is awaiting him," she concluded.

I didn't bother to counter the attack. I rejoined with only one sentence below her article on *The North American Tribune* website: "I wish that my bladder were larger than my ego so I could piss off more people of Yan Haili's ilk."

The story she referred to, the arrest of Sister Liang, was another investigation I'd been working on recently, and I would keep writing about it regardless of the fact that my reports might contradict the official findings. Though Sister Liang, a stocky, homely woman, had broken the law and pulled in millions of dollars from human trafficking, I suspected she was a scapegoat. There must have been more powerful collaborators who had given her name to the FBI. I had interviewed dozens of immigrants in Chinatown, Brooklyn, and Queens, and not a single person voiced a negative opinion about her. Some insisted on her innocence, some said they would visit her in prison, and some still regarded her as their benefactor. She had helped many people, especially newcomers who had landed in this city penniless and hapless, even as she had charged sixteen percent annual interest on loans. A young man I talked to said he still owed her eleven thousand dollars and didn't know how to pay it back now that she was in jail. The people of her home village, to which she'd donated a schoolhouse and a veterinary clinic, had sent a letter to the federal judge to appeal for her release. Nevertheless, the judge gave her seventeen years for being guilty of five of the six charges.

I knew Haili was angry at Sister Liang because she had lost her investment, probably tens of thousands of dollars, in the woman's underground bank, which had offered eleven percent annual interest on CDs but which had been shut down by the police for money laundering. In my reports, I mainly quoted others without putting in my views. Granted that the way I presented her story might have been a different take on the case, it was my job to let people hear different voices so that they could make their own judgments. They mustn't just accept the official verdict without question.

ON SATURDAY MORNING the city was fogged in, and I set out to see Niya. My 7 train stopped now and then due to delays and crossed signals. The train ran on an elevated track; I liked the view of the city in the fog, which smoothed out the untidy features of the rooftops and graffiti-covered walls. The city appeared serene, mysterious, less populated. I got off at Elmhurst, in Queens, and headed toward the café in which she and I were to meet and which offered breakfast and lunch and a variety of coffees. The soles of my boots crunched half-shriveled leaves as I plodded along the sidewalk. The late October air was milky and cool. A heavy-duty truck emerged, huffing like a boat plowing through water, while tendrils of ground fog curled away.

No sooner had I taken a seat than Niya appeared, wearing an off-white windbreaker. Wouldn't the color of her coat make her appear ghostly in the fog? Her roundish cheeks glowed with health. Seated with a square table between us and with her coat draped over the back of her chair, she ordered a cappuccino and I coffee and pancakes. She didn't want any food, saying she'd eaten breakfast already.

"Oh, it's so warm in here," she said and undid the top button of her tunic.

"You're quite cheerful today," I observed.

"Yes, I am in a bullish mood." Her smile dimpled her right cheek. "I just got promoted to associate director of the IT help center."

"Congratulations. Does this mean NYU will give you a raise?"

"You bet it does. You look out of sorts today. What's up?" She sipped her cappuccino, then licked the foam off her upper lip, which was shaded by downy fuzz visible only when it was wet.

I said, "I never thought I'd be labeled a separatist by the Chinese officials—Katie cannot get a visa on my account. I worry that I won't be able to go back to see my parents for a long time. My mother has angina and diabetes, and I'm their only son."

Niya breathed a feeble sigh. "That's why as soon as your tangle with Haili went political, I backed out. Politics is where I'm out of my element. Before my father died, he made me promise never to mess with politics."

"He died? Is your mother still living, or are you an orphan now?"

"They're both gone. I'm a twenty-nine-year-old orphan, still looking for a man and a home." She laughed but stopped short.

"You don't have a boyfriend?"

"I was dating a guy for a couple years, but he realized he was actually gay and broke up with me for an American man. He claimed he finally understood his sexual orientation and had to be honest with himself and with me. I think he has some trauma involving women—sometimes he said things that made me think he was abused by his mother or sisters when he was little."

"His masculinity was injured?"

"You have a nice way of putting it. You're like my father—he also had a way with words."

I laughed and realized we were enjoying each other's company, perhaps partly because we were both from the northeast of China. "How did your father die?" I asked.

"He died about ten years ago, of complications from AIDS."

"I'm so sorry. AIDS was very rare in the northeastern provinces at the time, wasn't it?"

"Still, there were victims. My dad had a stomach perforation and underwent an operation at a hospital in Harbin. They gave him a transfusion, but the blood was contaminated. Afterward he got sicker and sicker and was finally diagnosed with AIDS. We demanded that the hospital cover his medical expenses and pay damages, but they denied any responsibility. It was outrageous, and it wasn't an isolated incident—a number of women in labor at that hospital had also received contaminated blood and became HIV positive. My father was so outraged he couldn't stop cursing the hospital administrators. He went to Beijing to present a petition, but he was detained the day after he arrived and was escorted back to our home province." She paused and collected herself.

Then she went on, "They incarcerated him and wouldn't release him until he agreed not to go to the capital again. He filed a grievance with the local government, but officials all turned a deaf ear. So he wouldn't stop drinking and went downhill. When he was dying, he told me to leave China and never return. He even suggested I go to Siberia, where some of his acquaintances were doing business and running orchards and vegetable farms. He said, 'This is a country that devours its people. Go live elsewhere and don't mix with the Chinese.'"

"But your father was Chinese, wasn't he?" I asked. I was moved by her story.

"Yes, but many of his friends were minorities—Koreans, Huis, Manchus, Mongolians. He got along better with them. At one time he thought of fleeing China too."

"Where would he have gone?"

"Taiwan, perhaps, or Hong Kong or Southeast Asia."

"He never left?"

"The government wouldn't give him a passport. Even with

a passport in hand, I doubt he would have been able to leave because it would've been hard for him to survive elsewhere. Even though he hated the government, he was Chinese to the bone."

"So you have nothing to do with China anymore?"

"Believe it or not, despite everything, I still love our motherland."

"But you're naturalized, aren't you?"

"A U.S. passport makes my life easier, especially when I travel, but at heart I still belong to China. I love everything Chinese besides."

"But you don't seem to like Chinese men, do you?"

"Well, how should I put it?" Niya considered the question. "Maybe I've changed a lot since coming to the States. Sometimes I'm attracted to Chinese men, but whenever I spend time with them, I begin to feel uncomfortable and even annoyed. Many of them were spoiled by their parents and have huge egos. And so many of them are political animals that love power more than anything else. Their only ambition in life is to become a high official. They don't have any spiritual depth. They're pragmatic and self-interested. Oh, present company excepted, of course."

"I could be like that," I admitted, "or used to be. But it's the culture that shapes people in such ways."

"See, you're different, in a good way. Tell me, won't your girl-friend be mad at you if she finds out that you've spent time with another woman alone?"

"Especially a Chinese woman?"

Niya grinned, almost innocently. I noticed that she looked much better when she smiled—every feature on her face was in symmetry, and even her teeth were white and neat. I said to her, "Since we Chinese men don't appeal, do you want to marry an American man, like Haili did?"

"Well—" Niya pursed her lips. "I once dated a white guy, and it was hard for me."

"Why?" I was intrigued.

"This guy—he was an overgrown child. He wasted all his time in bars and playing games online. He made me feel like I was just his provider. I'm pretty sick of American men."

"I don't believe that most American men are like that," I said sincerely. "Some of them I know are quite warm and decent."

"They must be gay," Niya replied promptly. "Most good men in New York are gay."

"Heaven help me, you're so prejudiced! You can't just think of people in categories like that."

"I know I sometimes throw out clichés." She smiled as if to apologize. "Guess I've had bad luck with men. After I broke up with the white guy, I was too afraid to date anyone for a long time."

"Was he before your Chinese boyfriend or after?" I asked.

"After."

I had not expected she'd speak so personally and candidly. I confided, "My girlfriend, Katie, sometimes complains I'm too rational."

"That might not be so bad, though. At least one person should be clearheaded if a relationship is going to work. Are you two engaged?"

"No, there's no engagement."

"Have you thought about proposing to her?"

"Neither of us really believes in marriage, and we may never reach that point. But don't tell Haili this, all right?"

"I won't breathe a word," Niya promised. "But why are you and Katie still dating if the relationship isn't getting anywhere? I wouldn't plunge into something if I wasn't certain it would last."

"I just don't want to lose her," I said.

"Oh—" Niya smiled impishly. "I see why."

"Why?"

"Vanity. You want to show that just as Haili has a white husband, you can have a white woman. To prove that you've really made it here."

"Well—" Wounded, I began to protest, but then stopped. "I care about Katie, but there might be some truth to what you're saying. Like most men, I'm afraid of becoming a man nobody wants."

"But vanity cannot make a relationship last," Niya insisted. "Even if you two get married, the marriage won't be stable."

"Like Haili's, you mean," I said.

"Well, with her—I actually believe Larry really loves her."

"But he made her sign a prenup."

"That's commonplace among Americans," Niya said dismissively, "especially the rich. Larry has been generous to Haili. Look at the clothes she wears. I've seen designer bags in her wardrobe."

Her praise of Larry vexed me, so I said, "She just tries to look like old money."

"But Larry always provides for her."

"Then why have they broken up?"

"Actually," Niya said, raising an eyebrow, "she just moved back. She told me how Larry called her again and again, saying he couldn't sleep for thinking of her and that their apartment felt desolate. He couldn't concentrate at work because he was worrying about her. He begged her to come home or he might lose his mind."

"He seems quite devoted," I said drily.

"Very much so." Niya shrugged.

"What has Haili been doing these days," I asked, "besides smearing me?"

"Working on her movie script."

"You mean she's still at it?"

"Yes, she was very excited about the progress she'd made when we spoke last time."

"Obviously there's been no movie deal," I reminded her. "But I must admit I'm impressed that she can still concentrate, even under so much pressure from the media."

"Genius is concentration." Niya seemed very sure of herself. "She's a tough woman, can take everything in stride, and goes to great pains to get what she wants. She's also very thorough, down to the last detail. I don't know anyone like her."

"I wonder if I might turn out to be the only loser in this scandal," I said ruefully. "Sometimes the whistle-blower blows so hard he busts his own bladder."

She burst out laughing. The black waitress with wide-set eyes and a small waist came over again and placed the bill on our table. As Niya picked it up, I tried to grab it from her. "No argument, okay?" she said. "Remember I just got a promotion? Plus, you came all this way to see me."

I let her. Her revelation about Haili and Larry's reconciliation troubled me, because it meant that my ex-wife could be bolder in her dealings with me. For the rest of the weekend I felt pretty down, though I wrote an English-language article giving an overview of the scandal, about three thousand words. Early the next week I emailed it, with a pitch, to editors I knew at both *The New York Times* and *The Washington Post,* in the hope that one of them might run it. English-language newspapers and magazines paid many times more than those printed in Chinese. I knew a freelancer, a Dutchman educated in England, enamored of San Francisco and kung fu movies, who published long articles in *Forbes* and *The New Yorker* two or three times a year, and the fees he collected for those pieces were enough for him to live on. Usually he was paid more than a dollar a word. When I heard that for the first time, I was astounded, but later I came to know that was the standard rate among top-tier publications. But in this case, payment wasn't what I was after. I wanted the mainstream media to pick up the story of the novel; that could give me some leverage, some international help, in tackling those crooks. I had high hopes of seeing the *Times* or the *Post* swoop down on this cabal of three.

Yet an article in English might not affect Haili that much, because she went by a different name here, Heidi Yan, and her prep school would be unlikely to know about her misconduct unless someone alerted them. I'd been debating whether, once the article was out, to pop a copy into the mail to her employer with a letter enclosed, but that would amount to career assassination. So what? I was fighting a war, in which no scruples should apply.

Katie had gone over my English-language article and made three or four corrections. She said the piece was lucid and readable, but after I had sent it out, she warned me not to raise my hopes that it would see print.

FIFTEEN

On November 3, in the middle of a warm Indian summer, Haili's publisher, Jiao Fanping, appeared at GNA, sporting shiny tassel loafers, a navy blazer with wide lapels and a single brass button, a checkered tie, and a counterfeit Rolex. Despite his flashy outfit, he looked cheap. He claimed that he had come to New York on business and dropped by just to say hello to Kaiming, as if they had known each other for years. His sudden arrival unsettled my boss and Lucheng, but they took him to the small conference room at the eastern end of our office building. They asked me to join them.

After oolong tea was served, Jiao said, "I want to be open and aboveboard with you fellows. Tell me, why the hell are you so determined to ruin my business and reputation?" He twitched his nose and sparse mustache; above one corner of his mouth, there was a curved scar.

"We've just been doing our job," Kaiming answered, smiling coolly but without looking Jiao in the eye. "We have to report the news accurately."

I said to Jiao, "I read parts of Yan Haili's novel. How could you agree to publish such rubbish?"

"Let's not talk about my taste and judgment," he retorted. "Let's talk about how to solve this confusion or misunderstanding."

"I'd rather call it fraud," I said.

"It's a novel," Jiao replied calmly. "Fiction is supposed to be the work of the imagination."

"But you and Yan Haili have claimed that every part of the book is factual," I countered. "That's when it becomes fraud."

"Feisty guy. The fact is, you have a score to settle with your ex. But surely you know by now that you're not dealing with her alone. You've gone beyond bounds." His face turned puce, the flesh on his jaw knotted.

My temper was rising too, and I asked, "Are you threatening us?"

"Only you."

All this time Lucheng sat silently, looking grim and sipping his tea without lifting his gaze. I went on, "This is America and I'm a journalist. My profession requires me to be honest with the public and always report the truth. If I don't do that, someone else will take over my job. You can't just shut people up here."

"Don't try to sell me that crap." Jiao jabbed a forefinger at my face. "I lived in America for years, and I know what this country's like. This is a place where a man of color has no chance. The honkies might let you grow a little bit, but they'll always keep you under their thumb. The moment you grow bigger than they expected, they'll strike you down. So don't tell me a tale of honesty and freedom and justice. I went through enough abuse here to know those are just fabulous lies. In this place a scribbler like you can thrive only by slinging shit in the face of your motherland. You give the Americans what they want to hear so they can feel superior to us. But they'll never accept you as a real American—they'll never see past your Chinky eyes and yellow skin. Once a gook, always a gook. Don't even attempt to get above yourself. All you can do is malign your own people and talk about how backward we are. But once you run out of tall tales, the Americans will find another to replace you. And don't forget that we can always hold you accountable for your misconduct here. If necessary, we can turn you into a bum even in this so-called free land." Jiao's voice was getting more and more shrill, and there was a bit of foam on his lips.

Before I could counter him, Kaiming raised his hand. "Fanping, let's find a quiet place where we can have lunch and talk calmly, all right? My colleagues here have to work and shouldn't be disturbed."

"Okay, I wouldn't mind that," the visitor grunted.

Kaiming whispered that I should stay behind, and I nodded my agreement. I was not only angry but also rattled by my exchange with Jiao—I had to stay away to gather myself. The three of them left, all smoking Jiao's Panda cigarettes. They went to Duckling, a Thai place down the street. Though I knew Jiao had plenty of pull back home, his threat didn't bother me. I felt confident that he and his collaborators couldn't do much to hurt me here. I congratulated myself for having anticipated this kind of intimidation and getting naturalized as soon as I had held my green card for five years. I felt that for once I had outsmarted China.

With a squirt of ketchup, I hurriedly finished the ham sandwich I'd brought along for lunch, then headed out for a walk. I again went to the construction site on Crufts Street, where a small clubhouse was being put up. Beside it stood a row of mailboxes that resembled a low aluminum wall. The last of the four apartment houses had its roof now, and workers were busy installing windows on the top floor. A parking lot, just paved and marked with numbers, stretched alongside a driveway, sending up ripples of fumes in the sunshine. I spoke with a young Mexican worker by the name of Sergio for a while. To my amazement, he tossed out a word or phrase in Mandarin now and again, such as "no problem," "not bad," and "a little bit." He told me that he had worked in a Chinese restaurant for six years, washing dishes, peeling shrimp, cutting vegetables, chopping meats. He was going to leave New York when the Indian summer was over. "You can find work down South because people there still build homes in winter," he said, his large eyes smiling. "I hate the snow." He sucked in his breath as if some snowflakes had just fallen down his neck. He might go to Atlanta, where he said there were a lot of Mexicans.

At one twenty, I headed back to the office. In the distance, on the brownish beach, a band of young boys were roughhousing and showing off to one another, doing handstands and cartwheels. I wondered if they were cutting school. One of them could do back handsprings, two in a row, but when he tried a backflip he landed on his knees. Beyond them, seabirds were standing motionless or skittering along the edge of the frothing surf, fluttering their wings and tails. Every now and then the birds let out squawks. Two speedboats chased each other, drawing whitish wakes in the bay. A breeze was wafting over a whiff of stinking seaweed. In spite of the fall, the sea looked warm and inviting.

Kaiming and Lucheng were already at GNA when I returned; they both looked more relaxed now. My boss didn't say anything about their lunch, but later I asked Lucheng how it had gone. He shook his head and said, "Jiao is a pain in the ass."

"Why is he so angry at America?" I asked. "Did he really live here?"

"He did, on the West Coast. He lost his wife to another man there, so perhaps he has a number of reasons to be angry." Lucheng shrugged. "He still seems to want to do business here, in any case. He told us he was planning to start a publishing house in Brooklyn."

"To bring out books in Chinese or English?"

"Both."

"Do you believe him?"

"Hard to tell. He said he'd been looking for a representative in New York. Danlin, you shouldn't rile Jiao up anymore. We didn't realize he was such a loose cannon—he could cause a lot of damage."

"I shouldn't rile Jiao up anymore?" I said, appalled. It was a moment before I could speak again. "All this time," I said, "I've been following your directions—yours and Kaiming's."

"The situation is different now," Lucheng said patiently. "Kaiming said we might do business with him to expand our own publishing arm. Jiao is extremely ambitious, and so are we."

For the rest of the afternoon I kept mulling it over. It seemed clear that my boss was capable of cooperating with Jiao eventually. Just before the end of the day, Kaiming called me into his office and told me to be more careful when I wrote about the scandal. He stressed that I should continue to report on it, but with more restraint, and that I should avoid personal attacks. I couldn't help but wonder what Kaiming had promised Jiao, and how I could continue to do my work when my boss's loyalties were now divided.

That evening I got a message from my editor at the Writers Publishing House. My book of essays had been pulled from the list "due to instructions from above." She did not elaborate and just said she was sorry about the cancellation but couldn't do a thing. The two thousand copies already bound would have to be pulped.

Just like that. I was so stunned I didn't go to bed with Katie that night. She slept alone, swaddled in a woolen blanket. Through the opened door of my bedroom, I could hear her murmur from time to time. For hours I sat alone before my computer, thinking about all the hours I'd put into those essays—all the time I'd spent in front of this screen stringing words together to become a book. I hadn't felt a loss this keenly in a long time, as if my book were a person.

The next stroke came at work the following day, when we heard from *The Readers' Guide Weekly* that they would no longer reprint my articles, not even the vetted and modified versions that had passed through the censorship bureau in Shanghai. The editor at the weekly did not explain and just said that no article by Feng Danlin would be allowed to see print. It was official: I'd been blacklisted.

The Ministry of National Security and the Party's Propaganda Department maintain several lists, organized by degree of "unacceptability." The top one consists of names that can't even be mentioned in newspapers and magazines—these names are also wiped from the Chinese Internet. By their very nature, the workings of these lists are secret.

No one in the office was discussing the ban openly. Even though I didn't know for certain if I could fully trust Lucheng anymore, he was my best source of information. I asked him to tell me everything he knew about the blacklists. He sighed, then said, "I don't know which one of them you're on. The way these things operate is that they give you as little information as possible—they keep you in the dark, and let your own fear be your worst censor." He paused, then seemed to reach a decision. "When we got lunch the other day, Jiao Fanping tried to convince Kaiming to fire you," he told me quietly. "He said you were labeled an advocate of the independence of Tibet and Taiwan—a separatist—and a Falun Gong supporter. He said that to the Chinese government you were a criminal."

I let out my breath. "What did Kaiming say?"

"He doesn't seem willing to let you go. He told Jiao that he wouldn't want to get sued and there were employment regulations here, so he couldn't fire you without a solid reason."

I nodded, relieved for the moment. I said, "I wonder if he's really afraid of a lawsuit, or if he wants me to keep doing the dirty work here."

"You have to be careful, brother. Those bastards must be desperate—they could do anything. They already have."

By presenting me as a secessionist to the Ministry of National Security and the Propaganda Department, Gu Bing and Jiao Fanping had succeeded in killing my book. I needed to figure out how to respond.

The following day Kaiming told me that he had contacted some colleagues on the mainland, and found that any article that mentioned Feng Danlin, even in passing, was automatically blocked in Chinese cyberspace. That meant that no publication in China was permitted to reprint anything I wrote. I felt a grim satisfaction that I had ended up on the top blacklist. One magazine in Guangzhou even removed my name from a recent interview with a Hong Kong philanthropist that both Wenna and I had conducted in a hotel on Park Avenue. She was listed as the only interviewer, though she had just introduced the man formally and I had posed all the questions. I was crushed.

THE NEXT WEEK began with a large white envelope delivered to me at our office. As the strapping UPS man was pulling away in his van, I stood at my window, wondering where the letter had come from. The sight of the sender's name followed by "Esq." set my heart racing. I ripped open the envelope and began to read. The letter was a summons stating that litigation against me was under way and that I was being sued for half a million dollars in damages. The plaintiffs were both Yan Haili and Jiao Fanping, represented by a law firm in Manhattan, and they were suing me for libel. Though shaken, I wondered if they would actually spend the money for the lawsuit. They'd already poured so much energy into trying to silence me, but everything they'd done so far had been in the economy of favors and politics, not dollars and yuan. Jiao was successful in China, but I didn't believe he could afford the legal costs here. Once converted into dollars, the Chinese yuan, worth about twelve U.S. cents each, would not amount to much, and it was unlikely that Jiao would invest in litigation that might not guarantee a return. Haili didn't seem to have the means either—unless Larry had agreed to foot the bills.

I shared the summons with my boss. After reading it, Kaiming seemed relieved and smiled secretively. "I told you to be careful," he said. "It looks like this case might drag on for a while."

I didn't know what to say. I was angry about his assigning me the scandalous case and now abandoning me to face the charges alone. Then I realized that Kaiming was relieved because they were not suing GNA, which should have been included in such an action. Unlike an individual, a company would be more able to pay the damages should it lose the case. Isolated and unprotected, I was helpless in fighting the accusation alone. Probably Kaiming and Lucheng had worked out some agreement with Jiao Fanping when he had popped up here the previous week. I felt betrayed but said nothing, knowing GNA would never intervene on my behalf.

When I booted up my computer in the office and accessed my email, the newest message was from Haili. She wrote: "We're going to sue your pants off. You might have to borrow Katie's outfits."

Despite my panic, I responded immediately. "The public is still waiting to see the movie contract you signed with Panorama Pictures and also to see the translations of your great novel into thirty languages," I wrote, my fingers punching hard against the keys. "When does the Chinese edition come out? I will do a write-up, I promise. How about the English translation? Has it been delivered to the White House yet? Any feedback from President Bush? Don't forget to send him and the First Lady an autographed copy. Laura Bush is an avid reader of novels. How about the Nobel Prize nomination? Have you begun composing your acceptance speech yet? You should start considering what to wear for that grand occasion."

That evening I showed Katie the summons. I wanted to know if I should hire an attorney without delay. She said one of her colleagues, Rudolph Jones, had once been a trial lawyer and we should talk to him first.

SIXTEEN

Rudolph was a black man in his mid-thirties; he was compact and wore a restrained Afro and wire-rimmed glasses that complemented his delicate, intelligent features. He lived in Douglaston, an upscale area in Queens. His spacious living room was lined floor to ceiling with shelves of books and journals. At the far end of the room, next to the wide bow window, stood a large birdcage in which a parakeet perched, its feathers shiny and gray, its bill cherry red. On the other side of the window was a potted camellia, about five feet tall but without flowers among its glossy leaves. As soon as Katie and I sat down on a blue corduroy sofa, the bird squawked, "Hello, Luke wan' cookie."

"Quiet, Luke, you just ate breakfast," Rudolph scolded. "You'll get high cholesterol."

I glanced at a beer stein sitting on a bookshelf containing tiny chocolate bird-cookies. Does cholesterol level have something to do with sugar intake? I wondered. The bird hopped onto the other wooden perch in the cage and shook its wings, its head drawn in a little. Katie said with a smile, "Luke is being naughty again. Does he have a sweet tooth?"

"No, he just wants attention," Rudolph answered. "He ate lots of cornflakes and blueberries just now."

I gathered that the bird might feel lonely when its owner wasn't home. This place was very quiet, if not isolated. Through the east-facing window I could see only pointed cypresses and junipers in the backyard and the roof of another condo building. There were no roads or traffic in sight.

I showed Rudolph the summons from Haili and Jiao's attorney. He adjusted his glasses and started reading it while his bony hand lifted a cup of coffee to his lips. He smelled of piney shampoo. The previous night Katie had spoken to him on the phone, so he already knew the situation. The Oriental rug on the parquet floor displayed a mahout-led elephant, astride whose back a young couple sat, the young man wearing a turban and piping a bamboo flute while the woman tapped a tambourine over her head. Katie picked a few pistachios from a redwood bowl on the coffee table and began cracking their shells. She loved nuts, any kind, even water chestnuts and coconuts.

Rudolph put down the letter and gave a small sigh. I asked, "Do you know anything about this law firm?"

"I'm familiar with it."

"Is it a major one?"

"Not really. A middling firm, I would say."

"Rudolph," Katie broke in, "what do you think Danlin should do? Should he hire a lawyer?"

"They don't have a case," I said. "They lied to the public in the first place. They're already known as a bunch of crooks."

"They may not intend to win the case. They may simply want to harass you, or force you into a settlement."

"I make less than twenty-five thousand dollars a year and can file for Chapter Seven at any time," I said, using the expression that I'd heard on the radio the previous week.

"You mean you have no property or savings?"

"I live paycheck to paycheck and have less than one thousand dollars in the bank."

"Then you're safe." Rudolph laughed out loud.

Both Katie and I were puzzled. "What do you mean?" she said.

He told Katie, "Danlin might not need a lawyer and can represent himself. Actually, he should write to tell their attorney that he has no money and is not afraid of litigation."

"What will happen next?" I asked.

"They might drop the case, because they won't be able to squeeze anything out of you. People start lawsuits to get damages. If there's no money in it, nobody will bother. In the legal field, everything comes down to dollars."

"It's the same in every field," Katie said, shaking her head.

I said, "But Yan Haili's husband is in the financial industry, so he has significant resources."

"This letter doesn't mention him as a plaintiff," Rudolph went on. "Tell you what, I know someone who's still at that law firm and I might be able to find out something about this case. I can't promise any results, but I will try. Lawyers are not supposed to reveal this kind of information. In the meantime, you should write back, deny the allegation, and tell them you have no money and are not afraid of any charges."

Following Rudolph's advice, I wrote my reply, denying any act of defamation and stating that I would represent myself because I could not afford an attorney. I made it clear that they couldn't get anything from me, a poor man who just had a few changes of clothes, an old computer, a three-speed bicycle, four pairs of shoes, and about a hundred books. If they continued to pursue this suit, it would amount to publicizing the scandal and making a spectacle of themselves, so they should think thrice before plunging deeper into the litigation. I concluded, "You can beat a dead horse as hard as you wish, but it will not hurt anymore."

After mailing the letter, I made the summons the subject of my column for the next day. When the piece ran, it refueled the uproar. Many people wrote in, condemning the crooks and saying that the threesome should be the defendants, indicted for throwing dust in the eyes of the public. "This is a typical case in which the victimizer plays the victim," one person commented. "An ultimate insult to people's common sense!" another wrote. I noticed that this time there were few comments in the simplified characters, which confirmed that my writings were blocked online on the mainland, reminding me that Gu Bing and Jiao Fanping might have survived the crisis there. That upset me.

I GOT A CALL from the Chinese consulate about a week later. The caller was Tao Wuping, a vice consul, who had reprimanded Kaiming on the phone for our reporting on the Falun Gong incident five weeks earlier. I'd met this man before—he was very educated, very accomplished. He sometimes went to the UN building on the East Side to represent China—he spoke English fluently and some French and was savvy about Western etiquette.

He invited me to the consulate, saying he wanted to have "a heart-to-heart." I felt uncertain about this. What if they wouldn't let me out of the building? What if they interrogated me and beat me up? What if they forced me to sign something? Then I scrapped these thoughts. I was not important enough for them to detain, which might make a piece of news and unnecessary trouble for themselves. As a U.S. citizen, I was no longer in their grasp. So I agreed to come, and we settled on three o'clock the next afternoon.

Before I left for work that morning, I told Katie about my appointment—when and where it was. "If for some reason I don't come back," I said, sheepish about my suspicions, "you'll know something's gone wrong."

I hadn't entered the pale gray building at the west end of Forty-second Street for years. It was the same inside, though the old man with the turkey throat, once the receptionist in the front office, had been replaced by a soft-spoken woman in her early forties. Tao's office was on the third floor. He was reading a magazine when I was led in by his young assistant. At the sight of me Tao stood up and stretched out his hand as he walked over to greet me. I had always been struck by how short he was—he couldn't have been more than five feet. It's common knowledge that people of short stature are rarely found in diplomatic service. Ministries of foreign affairs as a rule employ people whose physical beauty surpasses the national average, since diplomats are the country's public face. For China to have made such an exception for Tao was extraordinary, and meant that his service must be invaluable. As I shook his hand, I could already sense his charisma.

"Congratulations, Comrade Feng Danlin!" He greeted me cheerfully. His voice was resonant and forceful, his eyebrows sloped down to his temples, and his hair was raven black, obviously dyed.

"What happened? Why congratulate me?" I asked. I sat down on a leather sofa, its arms decorated with brass rivets.

"You were just elected one of the top one hundred Chinese intellectuals of this year, ranked ninety-four."

"Oh! I didn't know the voting had finished."

"It's a huge honor—and just announced."

I was amazed that he, an official, had followed the grass-roots election. I said, "I'm only a journalist—you're a real intellectual." I knew his credentials well—he had earned a PhD from

UC-Berkeley and authored a book in English on international politics. A decade earlier I had seen a spate of articles about his return to China, an event about which the media made a fanfare. Tao was celebrated as a hero who, out of his profound love for our motherland, had declined a professorship at a private college in Chicago. After his return he started teaching at Nankai University in Tianjin, but soon he entered the diplomatic service and his career took off. Now, in his presence, I felt somewhat inadequate—Tao seemed completely at ease and in control, though at the moment I might have been slightly better known than he was.

His assistant stepped in and served tea and a fruit platter— tangelos, grapes, kiwis, pears, nectarines, even a couple of plum tomatoes. A flat-screen TV mounted in a corner was on mute, showing CNN news—a squadron of U.S. helicopters had just attacked an Al Qaeda cell in Iraq. I took a sip of the tea, which was Big Red Robe. "Great tea!" I said, jolted by a sudden surge of homesickness. I hadn't tasted such a fine tea in years. I swallowed the lump rising in my throat, surprised by my emotion.

Tao began to talk about the relationship between China and the United States, saying we had to help strengthen the ties between the two countries despite their occasional friction. I was nonplussed, unable to see what he was driving at. For much of his career, he had condemned the United States and advocated aggressive foreign policies, even declaring at one point that there would be a war between China and the United States in the Taiwan Strait. Why all this talk about cooperation between the two countries now?

Tao told me, "I've been following your coverage on the novel *Love and Death in September*."

"Is it a national project?" I asked tentatively. I still couldn't quite believe it was backed by the government, as Haili had claimed—so many of her claims had evaporated when they were subjected to the barest scrutiny.

Tao seemed surprised, then laughed. Looking me in the face, he said, "We couldn't possibly have initiated such a thing. But when the novel started encountering so much flak here, mainly from you, we felt we ought to intervene because the situation could soil China's image. That's why we want you to stop reporting on it."

"I've been reporting on it because there's a lot to report," I said. "This novel is a sham."

"You could say that," Tao said, "but believe me, the author truly intended to promote mutual understanding between the Chinese and the Americans. So we want you to wrap things up and move on."

"How can I abandon this story? It's of great public interest, and it's important news."

"Because the way you report it looks like mudslinging, and this story has been dragging on for too long. If it keeps snowballing, it could damage the relationship between the two countries."

"Isn't George W. Bush going to endorse the English translation of the novel?" I said matter-of-factly.

"That's just hearsay and might not materialize, we all know." Tao forced a laugh, his rectangular face crinkled a little. "Just let it go, all right? Danlin, you should learn to enjoy peace and harmony. Life is never easy—we always go from trouble to trouble. That's my definition of life—one problem after another until we die. Life is already hard, and there's no reason to create more difficulties for others."

"Let's be fair," I said. "I'm not the one who lied about this novel. If anyone is causing difficulties, it's Yan Haili and her publisher."

"Still," he said, "you can make peace."

"But a reporter is obligated to expose lies."

"I know you want to tell truth, but truth must serve a purpose. If it doesn't help make good, what's the point in telling it? I'm talking to you, Danlin, not as a Party cadre but as an older brother who has seen more and gone through more."

"I appreciate that, but I'm afraid I won't be able to comply." I was getting angry in spite of my calm voice. He was treating me as though I was supposed to be obedient and had to compromise.

"A smart man ought to know his place in the world. Have you ever thought about yours? Have you ever considered the odds you are facing? You're like a little turtle attempting to rock a boat shared by two huge countries. What will come of this? Clearly and simply, you won't be able to shake the boat at all, so you'd better give it a wide berth." His tone grew harder. "Also, keep in mind that you'll always be held responsible for your conduct, even here. If we draw a small circle on the ground for you, you'll have no choice but to dance around it for twenty years. If we put down a few more circles, your life will be wasted altogether. We don't have to deal with you directly—we can just put you in a category, and your value as a human being will be reduced to zilch. To a country like China, which has never been short of citizens, one person more or less makes no difference. Therefore, no Chinese citizens can afford to alienate themselves from our country. Think about what I just said. You don't have to respond now."

I was unsettled but managed to say, "Let me ask you something, Mr. Tao. Do you consider yourself an intellectual?"

"Yes, I do."

"Then why do you speak only for power?"

"I see this as my duty."

"Then my duty is different from yours."

"In what way?"

"I believe I ought to speak for the weak and the voiceless."

"Please be honest with yourself. We all know why you've been so aggressive—you have a personal stake in stringing out this case. Don't assume that the powerless are more decent than the powerful. People are the same, and there's no reason to create such a distinction."

"But one group is abused by the other."

"As I said, what you've been doing is seeking self-destruction while disturbing others." Tao touched a magazine on the table, *The International Forum.* "There's an article in this issue by Sam Waide, the prominent man of letters in the United States. Do you know his work?"

"Yes." I nodded. "I read his novel *The Woman I Left Behind* and enjoyed it immensely."

"Take this with you and read it carefully. You will see how an intellectual should define his role through serving his country. Sam Waide insists that American people ought to trust their president and give the White House a free hand so it can win the war on terror."

"But you're a Chinese," I said skeptically.

"I've been playing a role similar to Waide's, which is to combine my personal existence with the interests of my country and my people. If I serve, I serve our motherland. If I fight, I fight her enemies. I pride myself on my role as an intellectual of this type, because I know what the world is like and how it operates. Don't talk to me about justice, freedom, and equality. All those so-called universal values originated from colonialism and imperialism and have been utilized to suppress the local, the particular, and the colonized. Nowadays, at best they are abstract words thrown around to mislead people. They're merely beautiful lies. Tell me, at what point in history did the United States embody any of those values? It's true that people here have some freedom of speech, but their words are feckless, like farts. As a matter of fact, this country is the world's number one liar and hypocrite, yet we have no choice but to cooperate with it as much as we can because it's a superpower with more than a dozen aircraft carriers and thousands of nuclear warheads. The world is a battlefield where the strong, the winner, defines the terms of equality and justice."

"So to your mind there're no universal values at all?"

"Of course there are. But what's universal is not any of those abstract, misleading words."

"What *is* universal then?"

"Money. That's the universal language."

"This is quite cynical, isn't it?"

"It's the truth. Have you heard of the Great Firewall?"

"You mean China's Internet police apparatus in the making?"

"Correct. Who has been helping us build the system to regulate China's cyberspace? Some American companies volunteered. Because they all want a share of the Chinese market. They understand our policy—whoever is against us won't have any economic opportunities in China. Believe me, most people will sell their parents if there's enough profit to be made. History has proved that any of the Western countries will stop clamoring about human rights whenever China grants it a couple of lucrative deals. Money doesn't smell or rot and is invincible everywhere. So don't be misled by the slogans others chant. You must look at what they've done."

"Mr. Tao, I respect you as a scholar, but I must admit that

we're different species. What I want is to be an honest, independent, and rational voice."

"But I don't think you've been rational at all. You have confused your private life with your professional life."

"We both know that's not true."

"You're too stubborn—you treat everything in the world as black or white."

"What's wrong with that? One must have integrity."

"That's an American way to be."

"It's a positive quality the Americans have. Their first instinct isn't to compromise."

"That's why they wreak havoc. They're obsessed with abstract ideas and use them to measure everything and to shape the world."

"Without ideas there will be no vision. Without a vision, how can we improve things?"

"Don't assume you can become a real American. If you don't mend your ways, eventually you'll be ostracized and out of place wherever you go, and you won't be useful even to the Americans. When you're old, at best you'll end in a nursing home, toothless and incontinent, wearing diapers day and night, with no company but a small TV. Try to do some soul-searching and be honest with yourself. In this world no one can exist alone, detached from any group or community. No one can prosper for long by destroying their good relationships with others. It's always better to promote goodwill than to be a rabble-rouser. Now, take the magazine with you and think about what I just said. I hope one day we'll see eye to eye on something. By the way, have you seen this?" He pointed to a *World Journal* lying open on the coffee table, the page carrying an article about the daughter of Foreign Minister Liu—the girl had just been admitted to Yale.

"I read today's paper," I said, guarded.

Tao put his finger on the girl's fleshy cheek. "Do you think Yale accepted her purely for merit?"

"It seems unlikely."

"Right, they admitted her because she'll be useful to the university. By the same logic, you must make yourself useful to a country. That's how a person realizes his value. Without a country behind you, you'll be nothing. You're a smart man. Try to figure out how this young girl made herself useful."

"I don't think she herself is that useful, though," I countered. "It's her father who is important."

"That also makes her useful to Yale, doesn't it?"

"Well, I wish I had been born into a powerful family like that. Too late now. I can't blame my parents for giving me my humble origins."

We both laughed.

I left his office after another swallow of the fragrant tea. Though slightly unsettled, I must admit that I had enjoyed the exchange of words with Vice Consul Tao. Seldom could I have an invigorating conversation like that with Chinese officials; most of them just hemmed and hawed and appeared polite and mild to avoid expressing their opinions or confronting others. They were famous for showing no temper (immobile as a hill, not even batting an eyelid). Tao was an exception.

On the subway, I read Sam Waide's article, which was unconvincing. The writer argued that democracy could and ought to be exported as a civilizing mission of the West, so the occupation of Iraq was to establish the first democratic Arab country in the Mideast. It was also a way of stabilizing the region and maintaining peace and world order. People should therefore trust the professional politicians and allow the White House more time to make progress and eventually win the war. I was disappointed, because I liked Waide's novels, but this essay was narrow-minded and imperialistic. I could accept Waide as an intellectual, but he was not the type I wanted to be. I wanted to become someone who wouldn't hesitate to expose lies and hypocrisy or, if necessary, to speak against my country (if I still had one). Nevertheless, I understood that I had been chosen as a public intellectual mainly because people wanted to have honest voices in the media—by my qualifications, I wasn't an intellectual at all. All the same, now that I'd been officially voted in, I couldn't help brooding about this role and imagining how to fulfill it.

SEVENTEEN

Two days later I mailed the magazine back to Vice Consul Tao with a letter enclosed. I could not agree with him about serving one's country unconditionally. "What is a country?" I asked. "For me, it is not a mythical, sacred figure but an apparatus, like a set of machines (each ministry is a machine in this sense). It would be insane to regard the country as a deity and let it rule one's life. Moreover, I simply cannot trust any country, which might run amok at any time. That's why E. M. Forster hoped to have the guts to betray his country if he had to choose between betraying his friend and betraying his country."

I continued: "What if your country commits genocide? What if your country has become a fascist state? In such circumstances, a decent citizen should stand up to the government. History has taught us that no country is qualified for the moral high ground. An intellectual's role is not to serve the state but to keep a close watch on it so that it may not turn abusive, oppressive, and destructive. Therefore, as an intellectual, one must uphold justice, freedom, and equality as universal values. Abstract as those concepts might be, despite their problematic origins and despite the West's dubious history in measuring up to them, they are still essential in improving our social conditions and making us more human. Furthermore, I must emphasize that no true intellectuals should be in bed with power, letting political shifts determine their ups and downs, nor should they become the hangers-on of some lords. Vice Consul Tao, have you never dreaded the country you have been serving? Has it not destroyed millions of lives? Has it ever hesitated to swallow or squash even those who loved it? You claimed that without a country an individual would be nothing, but how many people have been reduced to nothing by their countries? *Patriotism* is a pejorative word in my dictionary: it connotes spiritual paucity, intellectual blindness and laziness, and moral cowardice. Isn't it terrible to let only a country form the underpinning of one's being? Last but not least, I don't believe that money is the universal value that you claim it to be—I don't believe that it can buy every soul and every thing. There are values beyond gold."

I had to write him to express myself clearly; otherwise he might have assumed I'd agreed with him. After the letter was mailed, I got more agitated. I knew the die was cast, and from now on the Chinese government would view me as an enemy. No matter what, I'd never be a servant of any country, because I believed that the country and the individual were equal.

About a week later Katie heard from Rudolph that the litigation against me was on a contingency basis, which meant that the attorney could get paid only after the case was won or settled. If the defendant had no money, all the effort would be wasted. This news heartened me. I could see that Haili had started the suit mainly to torment and intimidate me. Better yet, the contingency arrangement indicated that Larry was not financially involved. Rudolph told Katie that their attorney might discontinue his service unless the plaintiffs put up a retainer of eight thousand dollars. My gut told me that Haili was unlikely to take such a risk. She was always smart moneywise and wouldn't open her checkbook that way. On Katie's advice, I bought a bottle of Russian vodka for Rudolph.

Katie went back to the Chinese consulate to try again for her visa. To her delight, this time they granted it to her. The day after she'd told me the good news, I went to the visa office outside the consulate to try my luck too, hoping that my one-month-old U.S. passport would give me some leverage for a visa, with which I could accompany Katie to Henan province and visit my parents afterward. After standing in line for forty-five minutes, I reached a window in the visa office. The young man behind the glass skimmed the form I had filled out, glanced through my papers, and asked me, "Where's your Chinese passport?"

"I sent it in for renewal four months ago, but you haven't returned it to me yet," I replied. It was the truth. "I'm a U.S. citizen now. Why do you still need my old passport?"

"Because you're not a native-born American. See here, even your U.S. passport says you were born in China, in Jilin province, but without your original passport you cannot prove that. We have to confirm that you were a Chinese citizen originally."

"Can you check if my Chinese passport is still at your consulate?"

He punched his keyboard while reading the screen. He closed the small opening on the window and turned to speak to a middle-aged woman. His voice became inaudible. They both looked at the monitor, nodding their heads and commenting on something.

A moment later the young man opened the window and said to me, "We don't have your passport here."

"Are you sure? I mailed it to you four months ago. Here's a photocopy."

"This cannot prove we received it. We need the original."

"Damn it, you can't say I'm responsible for it disappearing!"

"Neither can we be responsible for that."

My head was reeling with confusion and anger, but I didn't know how to continue. I could only stare at his lean face.

"Well," he continued, "I'm not authorized to process your application if your papers are incomplete. Go upstairs, to Window Number Eleven, and see if someone there can help you."

I went to the second floor and handed in my paperwork to a bespectacled thirtyish woman, who said the same thing: without my former passport I couldn't possibly get a visa. "According to our rules," she explained, smiling all the while, "there's only one way for people in your situation to get a visa." Her smooth face brought to mind a fine porcelain vase.

"What's that?" I asked.

"We could give you a visitor's certificate—it can be used only once. Once you are back in China, you must report to the police department of your home province and cancel your Chinese citizenship with them. Then you come back and submit the official proof to us. After that, we will treat you as a regular American citizen and accept your visa application."

"But the fact that I've become a U.S. citizen already means my Chinese citizenship is canceled, because China doesn't recognize dual citizenship. You can easily verify the cancellation here."

"Rules are rules, and we have to follow them. You'll have to check in at the police department back home. They will issue you an exit pass, which you will use to return. Are you willing to do that or not? If you are, fill out this form, write your statement on this page, swearing that you will report to the police, and then give me four copies of your current photo." She handed me the form and a sheet of paper bearing the heading "My Affidavit." I was supposed to fill the page with a brief description of my situation and with a statement that I would present myself to the police once I was in China.

Driven by a sudden rush of eagerness to see my parents, I said, "All right, I'll do what you said and come back shortly."

She kept smiling. "See you later. You can take your photo downstairs." By now her moon face was quite friendly, the opposite of the standard officious face.

"Thanks," I said.

The instant I stepped away from the window, I realized there'd be no way I could turn myself in to the provincial police. Once I was in their clutches, I'd have to own up to my "misdeeds" abroad and might end up signing some agreement, or else they wouldn't let me return. They could coerce me into cooperation, even into working for them as a semi-agent or an informer. In brief, once I got into their precinct, they could close the gate and torture me at will, and I'd be like the deaf-mute whose protests couldn't be heard no matter how much pain was inflicted on him. I had a friend who'd once been imprisoned in Gansu province. The police were so brutal that they thrust a baton into his anus while stepping on his legs and forcing him to sing songs and curse himself. He was so traumatized that, even after fleeing China and going into exile in Western Europe, he couldn't stop talking about the humiliating experience—on the radio, on TV, to anyone who would listen. A little crazed, he would publicly declare that China, as an evil empire, must disintegrate into small countries, as Lao-tzu advocates in the *Tao Te Ching*.

Clearly, the so-called visitor's certificate was just a snare for the people on a blacklist. A jolt of fear hit me in the gut—it was so strong that my legs almost gave way. I dumped the forms into a trash can and left the visa office, my mind in a whirl.

Heading back to the subway, I kept saying to myself, "Fuck that! Fuck ruthless China!" Still, I was so saturated with grief that I could hardly breathe and my temples were throbbing. It had been drizzling, the neon lights along the street blurrier than three hours before, and my face was wet with both rainwater and tears, which I didn't bother to wipe away.

Despite my new misgivings about Kaiming, I told him about my visa problem the next afternoon—he had helped me with such things before, and with Haili's lawsuit now hanging over my head alone, I figured he owed me a favor. He listened attentively and then said, "In fact, there's still a way you can get a visa."

"How?" I asked eagerly.

"Find someone willing to vouch for you—someone who is at least a vice minister. This is a new policy. If you want to get a visa, you must have your name removed from the blacklist first, and nobody but a powerful official can help you with that. Of course, you'll have to write out a self-criticism to express your deep remorse and promise to toe the line. Keep in mind that they'll have the right to publish your confessions anytime they like."

My excitement faded instantly as I realized Kaiming had been talking tongue in cheek. He knew I would never accept those terms. I said, "So I'd have to behave here or I'd compromise my guarantor."

"Correct."

I made light of it. "Well, I don't know any big officials personally," I said, "so I'll just have to wait for the day you become a high official and can endorse me."

"No"—he laughed—"I would never do that for an incorrigible troublemaker like you."

I went into a deep funk. From now on I had to remain emotionally detached from China while trying my best to manage my pangs of loss and homesickness. As I had brashly advised in an essay: "Banish China from your mind."

In mid-November, Katie got another piece of good news. The Chinese Academy of Social Sciences had awarded her a fellowship that would enable her to live and do research in Beijing for six months. I knew she had applied to the academy's scholar exchange program, but neither of us had expected her to get it, because her kind of research was likely to expose the sordid underbelly of China's economic reform—the medical system in the countryside had been a shambles in recent years. Then why had Katie received the fellowship?

I wondered if strings had been pulled because of her relationship with me—whether the officials intended to separate her from me to make me more isolated, more vulnerable, and more distant from the mainstream media here. Without an American partner, I could be easier for them to control, and they must have believed that without her involved, the English-language media wouldn't pay attention to my work. That was merely my guess; I had no way to prove it. Yet I was certain that the consulate had issued her the visa with the intention of taking her away from me. (It's always more troublesome for the officials to deal with a foreigner, especially a Westerner. In general, they treat a Chinese who has a foreign spouse with some courtesy for the sake of good appearances.) Undoubtedly some officials had been in contact with Jiao Fanping and Gu Bing.

For days I was ill-tempered, full of misgivings about whether I should have engaged the trio to begin with. The anguish gave me bouts of indigestion, acid often shooting up my throat, and I would awake in the early morning hours, unable to go back to sleep. When I spoke to Katie, I couldn't help but get sarcastic. For a while she was able to ignore my nastiness. Then one evening she couldn't hold back anymore and snapped at me, "For Christ's sake, stop dumping on me like that!"

"Who's dumping who?" I spat back.

"Don't act like this is a surprise," she said softly. "I've never lied about my feelings. I told you from day one that I might decamp at any time. Besides, we can have a long-distance relationship, don't you think?"

"Okay, we can try that."

I wanted to say I needed her more than ever to be here with me, but I thought better of it, knowing there'd be no use. For her, the opportunity was too precious to let go and would eventually ensure the publication of her book, which in turn would help her get tenure. So much of her career hinged on the field-work she would do in China. I added, "I wish we'd never met."

"I'm sorry, Danlin." She spoke with so much sadness in her voice that I heard sobs behind her words. "If you meet another woman, feel free to be with her. I know I'm not the right one for you, but I'll remember you fondly."

I said nothing, afraid of dissolving into tears if I opened my mouth. How could I have become so sentimental? Hadn't I decided long ago that I wouldn't marry her? Why couldn't I just let her go? I realized that my feelings for her had changed considerably in recent months. I reminded myself to appear stolid and never to hold her back.

She had to work on a senior's thesis, so I turned away to watch the evening news. My eyes were on the TV, but I could hardly register what the anchorwoman was saying. I clicked it off and tried to read *This Earth of Mankind,* by Pramoedya Toer, a novel Katie had recommended to me. I had just started it and had been enjoying it, but now I couldn't lose myself in the story. The words crowded together before my eyes and refused to make any sense.

That night when we went to bed, I found myself unable to have sex with Katie. I held her in my arms, a strand of her hair between my lips, but I couldn't continue—a dull backache seized my body while a gust of grief rolled over my mind, dissolving my concentration. I closed my eyes and bit back my tears.

EIGHTEEN

At work the next morning, I again ran into Jiao Fanping. His navy blazer was flapping open as he walked over. Why's this crook here again? I wondered. He stopped to size me up, his triangular eyes glaring like a pair of tiny arrowheads. Then he turned and padded away down the corridor to Kaiming's office, his hands clasped behind his back. The moment Jiao entered that room, Lucheng's laughter rang out. I guessed that the three of them knew one another pretty well by now and were probably discussing the publishing business they planned to expand together in Brooklyn. Jiao's presence made me anxious, though he left within an hour. I feared that my boss might get too close to him. Sometimes Kaiming would act like a gregarious fool and make friends indiscriminately. I had tried reminding him to be careful, but he said networking was essential for our business.

Around midmorning, a hulking man with a shock of ginger hair arrived at our office. He introduced himself as Jay Trouton, from the Department of Homeland Security. He was so dressed up—in a dark blue suit, a red paisley tie, glossy wingtips—that with a visored cap on his head and less girth, I could have taken him for an airliner's captain. His full forehead, doughy face, straight nose, and muffin chin made me think of Ben Franklin. What a classic American face! I couldn't help but wonder whether he was descended from the founding father. My boss greeted Trouton as if he'd been expecting him and asked me to join their conversation, serving as the interpreter. Kaiming had a solid grasp of English, but once at a culinary competition he had made a roomful of people erupt in laughter by trying to say "cut to the chase" but instead saying "cut the cheese," and since then, he had always used an interpreter. Even when he spoke English with someone in a private group, his tongue seemed to grow stiff and wayward. As a consequence, he tended to avoid big words like *recapitulate, inconspicuous, osteoporosis, anachronistic,* which he used to be able to toss out with some ease and flair. Worse still, for a year after the "cut the cheese" fiasco, whenever speaking to an audience, he suffered stage fright, accompanied by facial tics and eye twitches.

Waving his fingers over a steaming cup of coffee, Trouton said he had come just to have a chat with my boss. Indeed, as I sat and translated, they didn't talk about anything serious at all. Trouton could speak a smattering of Mandarin and threw in a Chinese word or phrase from time to time, such as "so-so," "never mind," "no end of trouble." He had been to China two years before and liked Dalian the most, because its climate reminded him of his hometown, Boston. I thought that Boston was much colder in winter and more humid in summer than the Chinese coastal city, but I didn't interject. Kaiming said he loved Dalian too—an aunt of his lived there, working in a Pfizer plant that made animal health products.

I was puzzled. Why would an official like Trouton come just to chitchat with Kaiming? They went on to talk about the situation in China. "I was there three months ago," my boss told him, and I translated his words. "The country has changed so much that I felt like a foreigner when I walked down the streets. I was lost several times. Lord save me, the Chinese jaywalked at will, but I didn't dare to do that, and people laughed at me. They could tell I was from abroad."

"There's no doubt about the huge changes. Things are slowly

getting better there," Trouton said, smiling without opening his mouth, as if tasting something cautiously.

Kaiming went on, "But when I spoke with my neighbors and old friends, I found they were the same—their mind-sets hadn't changed at all."

"That must be true," Trouton agreed. "We should give them time. China's on the right track."

"Yes, slowly it's moving forward."

I was sure Kaiming understood Trouton perfectly, but he wouldn't respond until I'd finished translating—he seemed to want the extra time to think before he spoke. Their conversation shifted to the relationship between China and the United States. They both agreed that the two countries needed each other, actually depended on each other. "China has become an ally of a sort," Trouton said. Though taken aback, I rendered his words accurately. He stressed that as a U.S. partner, China was of course problematic and even troublesome, but there was no alternative—we had to work with the Chinese government in a mutually beneficial way. Surely we'd like to see a democratic China, but that was impossible for now, so we had to make do with what was out there, and not disrupt things by pressing the regime too hard. If the Chinese government collapsed, the world economy would suffer along with it, and there'd be famine and refugees everywhere, so, for now, the status quo had to be maintained.

I still couldn't figure out why Trouton was here. He seemed to be enjoying himself, but we were strangers to him and he was acting too friendly. Around half past eleven, Kaiming offered to take him to lunch, and he accepted the invitation readily.

Together the three of us went to the Thai restaurant down the street. Trouton ordered coconut chicken soup, saying he had to watch his weight. Both my boss and I had pad Thai. I'd eaten only a donut for breakfast, so I was hungry and wanted beef in my noodles, while Kaiming picked fried tofu, which he didn't often get to eat at home because his wife was allergic to soy products. Instead of the beers that the other two ordered, I opted for a mango puree. I was to continue to translate for them.

Our food came quickly. "This is excellent," Trouton said. His heavy jaw moved sideways as he chewed, pushing his cheeks with his tongue from time to time. Purplish veins like filaments were visible on his nose, and his nostrils were partly blocked with reddish hair.

He and Kaiming picked up the thread of their conversation about the relationship between China and the United States. Trouton said, "We understand that your agency handles news differently from the official agencies in China, and once in a while you give the Chinese government a hard time."

"We don't have to deal with censorship here," Kaiming replied. "We want to remain independent, but it's not easy. We believe in advocating some democratic causes, like the free election of village leaders in China's countryside and the Tiananmen Mothers." I explained to Trouton that the latter referred to a group of women who'd lost their children in the violent suppression of the student movement in 1989 and who had continued appealing to the government for a public apology and compensation.

"I can sympathize with you," Trouton replied. "But like I said, China is a country we cannot afford to alienate while we're fighting two wars. It has begun playing a major role in the international arena, and we need its cooperation now. So you guys ought to help us improve and strengthen our relationship with your country." He smiled, his greenish eyes twinkling.

I felt it odd that he used the term "your country," given that

Kaiming had been naturalized for years and called himself an American, and I had just received my U.S. passport. (My boss often mocked his patriotic Chinese friends, saying, "You know what? China is your illness, your heart problem, and your spiritual jailhouse. You'd better quit the drug of patriotism." His friends would fire back, declaring they didn't believe in the crap about world citizenship: "No matter where you go, you cannot shed your yellow skin.") I was pretty sure that Trouton knew we were U.S. citizens, but he didn't take us as his countrymen.

My boss sparred gently with him: "By *relationship,* do you mean 'friendship'?"

"Well, you could put it that way."

"In fact, we all want to see the two countries get along," Kaiming continued. "Together China and the United States can make the world a better place."

"I'm with you on that, a hundred percent. Keep in mind that the two countries will stand together on many major issues for a long time."

"That's what we want to see too."

"People in the same boat must help each other," Trouton said and raised his spoon, revealing a silver cuff link. I was amazed he knew that expression.

Trouton offered to pick up the tab, but my boss handed his credit card to the waitress before she showed us the check.

"Thank you for the delicious lunch," Trouton said amiably on our walk back. Pressing his left hand on his chest, he added, "Next time lunch will be on me."

Would he come again? I noticed Kaiming smile pensively, his cheek twitching.

MY BOSS WAS BESIDE HIMSELF after Trouton had left in his Ford Crown Victoria. I couldn't see why Kaiming was reacting this way. "You don't understand politics, Danlin," he said.

"You mean the Department of Homeland Security has targeted us?" I asked.

"Not only that. The White House and the Chinese government are working in tandem now."

I couldn't believe it. "Come on, this is a free country," I protested, "and it's not like we've broken the law. We've done nothing wrong."

"Free country, my ass. That man came here to warn us not to do anything rash that might damage the Sino-U.S. relationship, especially before President Hu's visit to the States next spring. We're in Trouton's charge now, and he will continue to scrutinize and handle us."

"But he said nothing like that."

"He didn't need to! His presence here was enough to get the message across. Obviously they've been handling us in the Chinese way—he uses his appearance here to rope us in. Danlin, you're so innocent, still a virgin in the whorehouse of politics."

"You might be right."

"I *am* right." Kaiming sounded impatient. "Look at what China's been doing. It has kept its backyard—Afghanistan and Pakistan—open to the U.S. in the past twenty years. Originally it was the U.S. and China together that created the Islamic militants there to fight the Soviets. In the eighties China sent PLA officers to train those fighters in guerrilla warfare and also provided them with light weapons and tens of thousands of pack-horses, while the U.S. gave them millions of dollars and Stinger missiles that brought down hundreds of Russian aircrafts. Then the Soviet Union collapsed, but the militants became the genie out of the bottle, plaguing the region. Now the U.S. and China have no option but to join hands to deal with all the blowback of violence and terrorism. China may need the U.S. to occupy that area so the militants in Xinjiang Uygur won't have their foreign bases across the border anymore. The two countries have a lot of common interests in Central Asia."

"Still, they don't share the same values," I said, not entirely convinced by his logic.

"That's high-flown rhetoric. As far as countries are concerned, only national interests dictate their union and separation."

"But I have a suspicion that China and the U.S. might not get on in the long run."

"They will, believe me. They're bound together. China has become a large U.S. factory, so the Communist regime will remain in place for many years unless China miscalculates and challenges America's supremacy."

I shook my head. "What you're saying sounds something like a bad marriage neither party can get out of," I said. "But even a married couple can divorce at any time and become strangers or enemies."

"It's not that simple. I'm quite sure that the two countries will be partners for a long time. China must've demanded that the U.S. side rein us in so its image won't be tarnished here. Some people in Beijing even believe we can influence the U.S. Congress. Jiao Fanping and Gu Bing must have done a hell of a job in presenting us as major troublemakers to the Chinese government. That's why Trouton came to warn us. From now on we have to do our best to stay friends with him. I never thought we'd have to deal with the U.S. government as well."

"Don't worry so much. Let's just keep our eyes open and see what happens next." Feeling it preposterous that the official's visit would rattle him so much, I said, "Why are you so afraid of Trouton? He's nothing compared to the Chinese officials we've dealt with."

"Are you simpleminded or what? I know how to handle those Chinese bastards. I know how to bribe them. But you can't bribe someone in the Department of Homeland Security or the FBI."

"You mean American officials are clean?" I said skeptically. "I'm positive some of them take bribes too."

"But I don't know how to grease palms the American way and dare not run the risk."

"I never thought our investigation of Haili's novel would anger so many people," I said wearily. "She said her book was a national project, endorsed by the Chinese government, but Vice Consul Tao denies it."

"It might be true only in the sense that one or two high officials support it. Those sons of bitches in power are idiots and think that they can buy off the United States with a couple of candy bars. They don't understand that this superpower has to be fed with billions of dollars continually."

"So Haili's novel is just a candy bar?"

"Or a cookie at most."

I broke into a laugh, and Kaiming followed suit. He then wagged his chin as though to awaken himself fully. I had the feeling that he might have withheld something from me, so I couldn't share his anxiety completely. He was a sharp man and could sense danger ahead of time.

NINETEEN

The apartment houses on Crufts Street were completed, all wrapped in simulated wood siding, fireproof and durable. Because of the sluggish real estate market, the builder was renting out the units as well as selling them. Both FOR SALE and FOR RENT signs were planted alongside the driveways. On my way to work the next morning I bumped into Randy. He wore a brown leather jacket and was walking with his head bowed a little, as though deep in thought. His sandy hair was tousled, and he had three or four days' growth of beard. I got off my bicycle and greeted him to see if he still remembered me.

"Hi, Danlin," he said, shaking off his reverie. "How's it going?"

"Not very well," I admitted. "Do you remember that conversation we had, about my carpentry? Would you still hire me as a carpenter when there's an opening?"

"Only if you're good. You need to show us you can do the work first, then we can decide whether to take you on. But winter's coming, and new construction won't start until next spring."

"I understand," I said. "I'm a decent carpenter, you know."

"Do you have a work permit or a green card?"

"I'm a U.S. citizen," I said proudly.

"Oh, I'm sorry," Randy said hastily. "I shouldn't have assumed."

"I just got my citizenship," I assured him.

"Well, congratulations then." Randy reached out to shake my hand. "Stop by every once in a while."

"Thanks. This means a lot to me."

"No sweat, buddy."

He walked off, an accordion folder stuffed with paperwork tucked under his arm, and he passed over the spot once occupied by a pair of blue Porta Potties. Beyond him, beech saplings, all about six feet tall, stood, their trunks whitish in the sunshine. I had his business card in my drawer. These days I could not escape feeling insecure at GNA. At night I kept dreaming of strange infants, small people—some of them stretched out their miniature arms, inviting me to hold them. According to Chinese folklore, this might be an insidious omen, and it made me consider the possibility of working for Randy's company.

Kaiming sent for me as soon as I arrived at work. I shucked off my peacoat and went to his office. As soon as he saw me, he crumpled up a sheet of paper and dropped it into his wire wastebasket. He looked frazzled, his eyes tired, his face drawn. Without question he'd slept badly the night before. He was in his white shirtsleeves and gestured for me to sit before his desk. I plopped down in a chair and crossed my legs. Behind him on the wall was a tasseled banner, presented to GNA by a charity association and emblazoned with these characters: *Let truth shine in words!* To Kaiming's left, a pair of olive-green filing cabinets stood against the wall.

"Danlin," he said, "I need you to take a leave."

"What?" My hands gripped the chair. "You mean I'm laid off?"

"No, no!" He shook his head and gave a little laugh. "Good heavens, you're a nervous wreck too. I mean I'm sending you out of town on a paid leave."

I relaxed my grip on the chair. "For how long?"

"A week."

"Why? Whose way am I in?"

"We're facing pressure from the officials on all sides. It's best for you to get some physical distance from the situation."

"Fine," I said, warming up to the idea. "I could use a break."

Kaiming nodded, looking relieved. He said, "Can you go to Berlin? There's a festival there this weekend, celebrating Chinese culture. Some well-known artists will be exhibiting their work, and you can cover it."

"I'd love to go, of course," I agreed, despite knowing the festival might not be very exciting.

Not only was this a chance to travel, but it was also, I realized with some sadness, a way to get away from Katie for a while. She'd already begun preparing for her trip to China. If I was around, I might get nastier. She planned to stay in China for the whole spring semester and part of the summer. I felt we might part ways anytime if she met another man there. Our fruitless relationship seemed to have been wasting my life, and lately I'd been longing to settle down and start a family, to live a peaceful life, though I was still unsure if I would marry. But now that I knew I wanted children eventually, I recognized I should entertain the possibility. In my heart of hearts I knew I wouldn't want to become a perpetual bachelor, an "old boy." If only I had some money saved up.

I was eager to use my U.S. passport for the first time. I knew people who'd gone to Toronto soon after naturalization just to see for themselves that they could cross the border into Canada and back without trouble. Kaiming had a niece studying at Dalhousie University in Halifax, but the girl couldn't come to see him because she held a Chinese passport and dreaded the tedious and frustrating process of visa application. The previous fall, Kaiming's sister had gone from Shenzhen to Nova

Scotia to see the girl, and hoped to make a stop at New York, but she couldn't get a visa in advance, so Kaiming had to fly to Halifax to see them in spite of his hectic schedule. Afterward, he kept telling others that only when Chinese citizens could go to 150 countries without having to obtain visas ahead of time would China truly be a strong country. He'd say this in jest, even to some Chinese officials' faces. Whenever someone countered that China was already a superpower, he would respond, "No, no, no, they still have a long way to go. Not until China has Japan's universal health care, Germany's free education, the Netherlands' paid parental leaves, America's open-stack public libraries in every town, and a world-standard passport for its citizens can China be called a global power." As it was, a Chinese passport allowed its holder entry into only a dozen or so small countries without a visa.

When I mentioned my leave to Katie, she said my plans were extravagant—who drops everything to take a vacation in Germany in late November? I said it was also a business trip that wouldn't cost much. Besides, GNA would reimburse my expenses. There was a network of Chinese-run hostels throughout Europe, and the lodgings were very affordable, usually under twenty euros a day, breakfast included. If Katie had come with me, we'd have had to stay at a regular hotel, which would cost three or four times more. I quickly found one of those hostels in Charlottenburg, a town outside western Berlin. The owner of the place, Mr. Huang, assured me that his house was absolutely convenient for everything and near the S-Bahn, the train that could take me anywhere in the city. I made a reservation and paid a fifty-dollar deposit with my credit card.

TWENTY

"Why are you coming to Germany?" the russet-haired officer at customs asked me while examining my passport. "For sightseeing and a meeting," I said.

"How long will you stay in the country?" he continued.

"A week."

He stamped my papers and let me through. It was as simple as that? I was still marveling over it as I wheeled my luggage out the frosted-glass door. What a privilege it was to hold a Western passport!

But my amazement made me pensive. I imagined two babies, one born in China and the other in the West, given different passports at birth—one child was automatically granted the freedom of travel. Why should the Chinese child grow up without the same right? What or who was responsible for that child's deprivation? The country the child was born into. A country that cannot endow its citizens with the same right of travel and migration as most other countries have, a country that makes its people second-class citizens in the world, has failed and should be held accountable by its populace. So much of our humiliation and resentment toward the West in reality originated from the country we created but cannot hold responsible. We allow the country, which should be the guardian of our rights and interests, to rule and abuse us like a god.

I made a mental note that next time someone argued against

universal values by insisting on China's particularity, I'd bring up this inequality as evidence that by overemphasizing our differences, we reduce our humanity—we must fight to have the same rights as everyone else in the world.

Mr. Huang's place was nestled at the end of an alleyway close to the train station. It was a three-story house that had a steep roof bulging with dormer windows; his family lived on the ground floor, and the other two floors were for guests. Because it was the off-season, I had a large room furnished with three beds and a few sticks of furniture, but such a big room felt lonely at night, in spite of the moonbeams sneaking in through the slats of the window blinds.

There were only four guests in the entire hostel, myself included. The others were a Korean student and a young Chinese couple who had come to Germany for sightseeing. The couple had just finished their master's degrees in civil engineering at the University of Manchester and were returning to their home in Suzhou the next month, while the Korean student, a willowy young woman named Doona Kim, was studying music in Vienna, where she said there were many Korean music students. Doona, with youthful candor, told us that she wanted to marry a European before her visa expired so she could live in Europe permanently. I joked that I hoped she already had a prospect, but she said she didn't yet.

Mrs. Huang, a plump Korean woman with permed hair and a batik apron, was from Yanbian, the Korean autonomous region in northeast China, and that was why they received some Korean guests as well. Because I was from the same province, the Huangs called me a fellow townsman. I enjoyed their lavish homemade breakfast, which consisted of kimchi, pickled string beans and soy sprouts, daikon slivers mixed with paprika and baby shrimp and squid, salted duck eggs, fried peanuts, rice porridge, and steamed plaited buns. I hadn't eaten this kind of breakfast in years. When I'd been a reporter back in China, I used to go to the Korean region at least twice a year.

I took the S-Bahn downtown to the Festival of Chinese Culture. I loved the German trains—they were clean, quiet, and punctual. Some were brand-new, still smelling of new metal and plastic. On my first ride I didn't realize that I needed to activate my ticket, but the conductor didn't fine me. She told me that if I were not a new passenger, I'd have had to pay forty euros. "But how do you activate a ticket?" I asked. She explained, but I couldn't understand everything she said. After stepping off the train, I stood watching people on the platform insert their tickets in the small red metal boxes to mark the time, till I learned how to do it.

The festival at the House of World Cultures, as I expected, wasn't very impressive. In addition to an assortment of paintings, photographs, and slide shows, there were theatrical performances, readings, and talks. Most of the folk plays had a single act performed by one actor because it was too expensive to fly in whole troupes from China; as a result, the performances were simple and at moments crude. I did not enjoy the readings and talks either. The literary events felt insubstantial, perhaps because most of the readings were done by German translators and actors on behalf of the authors themselves. I couldn't understand the German and felt disengaged. What I looked forward to was the small reception in the evening, at which I planned to interview some artists and officials. But because the German host had allowed a dissident poet living in London to sit on a panel that afternoon, the Chinese ambassador declined to appear at the party.

The German organizers were excited about Ambassador Chang's absence and congratulated the middle-aged poet for his power to nettle the top Chinese diplomat. The bearded poet only shrugged his thin shoulders and looked bemused. He was still holding a long-stemmed red rose that had been presented to him at the end of his reading. I asked him a few questions, to which he gave such terse answers that I could hardly quote him. He held out his glass to a bartender for a refill of red wine. Three waitresses were carrying trays of hors d'oeuvres around the room: pan-fried wontons, shrimp dumplings, spring rolls, sweet-and-sour chicken fingers, steamed shu mai, eggplant boxes, and pot stickers stuffed with crabmeat and zucchini. The food was excellent, sometimes even exquisite, but for this occasion I felt uncomfortable about all the appetizers. It was as if Chinese cuisine could always outshine our other arts, as if ours was a culture that satisfied only the stomach.

A bespectacled German man introduced himself to me in English as Stefan. He was dressed in a black suit, a lavender grosgrain tie, and cap-toe oxfords; the top of his head displayed a bald patch surrounded by curly hair. When he learned who I was, he was eager to talk with me about his work—he'd been writing a long article on contemporary Chinese literature. I was impressed by his knowledge of the subject—he seemed observant and erudite. He'd been involved in selecting the authors for the festival, and for that he'd had to read many novels. I asked him, among all the novels he had read, which one impressed him most. He shook his head and said, "None." Swirling his zinfandel, he confided, "We've spent more than a million euros for this series of events. I doubt whether it's worth it."

I didn't know how to respond.

I noticed that Stefan got his glass refilled frequently. He said he liked the California wines because he could taste the sunlight in them. I wondered if that was nonsense since I'd never tasted anything unusual in those wines. At the end of the reception, he invited me to his home nearby—he still had some questions for me, if I would oblige him. Though somewhat reluctant, I agreed after he assured me that it would be easy to catch the train back to Charlottenburg.

Stefan's apartment was crammed full of books, even the living room divided by rows of bookshelves. The moment I sat down, he left the room while his wife, a tall Lithuanian woman, poured me a cup of pekoe tea and placed a plate of rolled wafers next to it. Stefan came back with an armload of books. He put them on the glass coffee table and said to me, "These are the German translations of contemporary Chinese novels—I read them all in preparation for the festival. Please take a look."

All the novels on the table were well known in China, and I tried to think of what to say. Stefan went on, "I want you to tell me honestly: Do these writers accurately represent Chinese literature today? Or are they just some authors we Germans picked according to our own preference?"

I looked through the dozen or so titles again and found all of them were by the frontline writers in China, so I said, "These authors are major names and are regarded as the best ones writing now."

Stefan sighed and said almost inaudibly, "That country has more than a billion people."

His wife, a kind-faced thirty-something, piped in. "I read some of them. They're interesting. Stefan is a critic—more of a stickler."

Why was I feeling uneasy, even a little ashamed? Why should I care? I was not a fiction writer and no longer held a Chinese passport—why should I give a damn about those novels and what some Germans thought of them? Was Stefan an arrogant prig? Or was he a competent critic, sincere and knowledge-able in his judgments? It was hard for me to decide. He seemed well-meaning.

Those questions continued to nag me even after I had returned to Mr. Huang's house. I regretted not having explained to Stefan that those writers, every one of them, were talented but had to toe the line, not only on the page but also in their imagina-tions, because they received salaries from the state and could not afford to jeopardize their livelihoods. I wondered whether Ste-fan would have shown sympathy or contempt for my explana-tion. Most Westerners didn't have a clue how harshly and subtly censorship worked on an artist in China, whose talent, however prodigious, ultimately became docile and atrophied.

The next day, after filing my article on the festival with GNA, I went downtown again for some sightseeing. It got gloomy quite early in the afternoon, so after a late lunch of curry wurst in the Zoologischer Garten, I returned to the Huangs'. Berlin's winter could be depressing—the daylight was short and the air foggy. I thought of going to a concert by the Berlin Philhar-monic, but I was told that the tickets had sold out long ago.

A computer that the guests could use sat in the Huangs' study. When I scrolled through my emails on Tuesday night, among business exchanges and spam I saw a message from Niya. She wrote: "Danlin, I have news for you, but I should deliver it in person because I can't make much sense of it. Can we meet tomorrow or the day after?" She added a smiley face.

I answered: "Of course, I would be delighted to see you. I'm in Berlin on assignment right now—I wish we could meet here! I found an excellent Chinese restaurant in the center of Charlot-tenburg. They have amazing wheaten food. But I'll be back in New York in a few days and we can catch up then."

The restaurant was actually on Kantstrasse. It was called Melina, an unusual name for a Chinese restaurant. The exotic name must have been intended to make the place stand out as one that served the authentic cuisine of western China. According to Mrs. Huang, it had opened just a month before.

Amazingly, a few minutes later Niya's reply arrived: "Berlin!? I love that city and can meet you there. I can take Friday off. I've earned tons of miles with Continental Airlines and the flight won't cost me anything. My Turkish friend Aylin lives in Wannsee, and I can stay with her. Do you want to see me? Should I fly out?"

I reread her message, trying to figure out what she hadn't put into words. She didn't ask why I was away from New York, and she must have assumed I was here alone. She must have been to Berlin before and be quite familiar with this city. I'd always taken her to be somewhat like myself, still unaccustomed to the rootless cosmopolitan life that circumstances had thrust upon us. Now she seemed to be a savvy traveler. I remembered she had once mentioned she was kind of obsessed with travel and often left New York on long weekends. I had thought she just went somewhere in the States—Las Vegas or Yellowstone National Park or even West Point. Now I realized she must be an international traveler.

I took a few moments to gather my thoughts, and then wrote back: "Do come if you can. I would be happy to see you in Wannsee, which I am told is a wonderful area. I've finished my assignment and just been sightseeing. I'll be back in New York next Monday." I didn't ask about the news she had for me, because I understood she might not want to have a written mention of it. I gave her my phone number here in case she decided to come.

The Huangs had a daughter who was attending the University of Potsdam, a school just a few years older than herself, according to her. She majored in philosophy and still could speak some Mandarin but had forgotten how to read or write in it. She and I spoke English, which she had learned at the gymnasium. Unlike her heavyset mother, she was a string bean of a girl with walnut-shaped eyes. She had a German boyfriend, Andreas, who came to eat with us in the evenings. After dinner the girl and the boy would stay in the study doing schoolwork or just shooting the breeze. They smoked in there as well, which her parents allowed. They rolled their cigarettes with tobacco slivers from a pouch and folded tiny filters into the ends of the paper tubes. I chatted with them and discovered that Andreas's parents were Russian Jews. He'd been born in a small lumber town outside Vladivostok and had come to Germany when he was nine. At home he still spoke Russian, and he used to go to Jewish school on weekends but had quit that years before. "I have to work hard to get my diploma in computer science," he told me, his widow's peak touching his eyebrows. He'd also been learning more English, in which all the software manuals were written. Unlike his girlfriend, he was attending a vocational school. He loved to spend time at the Huangs' and often stayed late into the night.

Mrs. Huang told me in perfect Mandarin about her daughter. "We pay her tuition and give her food and a roof, but she must make her own pocket money by tidying rooms on weekends."

"She has a good boyfriend," I said.

"What can I say? She's grown up now. There's no way we can dissuade her once she decides to do something."

"You don't like the boy?" I said, surprised.

"That's not it. It's just too early for her to have a boyfriend."

I once conversed with the daughter alone and was impressed by her intelligence and sharp tongue. The girl no longer viewed herself as either Chinese or Korean, nor did she miss China, which she'd left at seven. She said she preferred a European rural town to a city like Beijing or Shanghai or even Hong Kong. "I wouldn't want to live in any of those cesspools," she said, waving a lean cigarette and puffing out smoke. I reminded her that many Chinese were getting rich, and that those cities she loathed so much had become hubs of opportunity where even Europeans flocked. She responded, "I don't want to make lots of money. I just want a quiet, quality life." I didn't know how to counter that; I supposed that everybody was entitled to their little portion of personal happiness. The girl seemed to be a spitfire.

In contrast to her, her father followed events in China avidly, reading the news on several major Chinese-language websites at least twice a day. He happened to know my name and said he enjoyed my essays and was honored to meet me in person, though he'd never thought I was under forty. "You're practically a young man," he said. "Amazing, tsk tsk tsk."

"You pictured me as an old fart?" I asked, laughing. We were both seated on the canvas sofas in the living room. "Tell me, Mr. Huang," I went on, "how long have you lived in Germany?"

"Eight years. Before this place we were in France and Italy."

"Do you speak French and Italian as well?"

"Only some French."

"Do you like it here better?"

He lifted his cup of aster tea and took a swallow. "A little better, I'd say. There're so many Chinese in Paris and Milan that it's hard to make a living in those cities."

"Have you been back to China?"

"No, I left more than twenty years ago, and later my family

joined me in Italy. My parents have died, and there's nothing for me to return to."

"Don't you miss home?"

"Of course I do, but I can no longer tell where home is. That's why my wife and I opened this guesthouse. We don't make much from it, but we like meeting people from China and Korea. This makes our life less lonely. A busy bee knows no sorrow, like the saying goes."

I could see that they couldn't earn much profit, given their rate, fifteen euros a day. In the off-season they also offered dinner for an extra two euros. How could they make money by charging so little? I said, "If you had your pick between Europe and China, where would you prefer to live?"

"Our own country, of course. But our country is a cruel place—it's like a crazy parent who enjoys torturing you until you lose your mind and your sense of being human. We can no longer live in China—once you leave, you leave for good."

I feared he was right, but asked, "Why so?"

"Because you begin to see other places and think differently. You have choices now. Who wouldn't choose a safer and more reasonable place to live?"

"Do you think Europe is a better place than China?"

"On the whole, yes."

"No prejudice, no mistreatment?" I pressed.

"Of course there is," he acknowledged. "There's plenty. But in the West, especially in Germany, society works by codes. Every profession has its codes. There are architectural codes, educational codes, legal codes, hotel codes, even restaurant codes. So you know what to do and what not to do. Even the powerful have to follow the codes, and they cannot bully you as long as you haven't broken any of those codes. This makes life easier and safer, especially for ordinary people like us. All we want is a life without interruption, today similar to yesterday and tomorrow similar to today."

He went on, "In China, there're good rules, but nobody follows them. As a result, rules don't mean a thing there, and an important person can bend the rules on a whim. This makes life unbearable for common people. When my wife went back two years ago, she saw how everyone there tried to take advantage of the little power in his hands—even a clerk at a small train station wouldn't sell her a berth ticket unless she received it as a personal favor, for which she'd have to do something in return." His voice grew frustrated. "How can you live comfortably in a place like that again after you've seen how people in other countries live and work? But for me, from my own experience, the worst part of life in China is that you must radiate menace to survive. You must be able to hurt others, to do damage with anger and bluster, or anybody can push you around. That's why people there seek power any way they can. An honest, kind-hearted person is nothing but a doormat."

"Isn't that the same everywhere, unfortunately?" I said, mainly to keep our conversation going. "People take kindness and honesty for weakness and stupidity. In America there's this saying—nice guys finish last."

"But in China this mentality of radiating menace is so prevalent that it has created a culture of paranoia and distrust," he insisted. "It has become a condition for survival, and it can drive you out of your mind. You have to be alert to danger constantly and cannot relax, because people around you are all radiating menace as well—everyone's afraid of becoming a clay pigeon for others to shoot. They all believe that even the devil would be afraid of meanness—the meaner you are, the better chance of survival you have. If I'd lived there longer, heaven knows what awful things I might've done. All that malice and sadness could have turned me into a wicked, spineless man. It's impossible to live an honest life in a place of fear and hatred. Now, how long have you been in the United States?"

"More than seven years," I answered.

"What's that country like?"

I thought for a moment about what to say. "Similar to Europe," I said, finally, "in terms of the codes you mentioned."

"Then it must be a good place to live." His mottled eyes glazed over. He took a gulp of the tea, his cheeks somewhat hollow, his perspiring scalp dotted with age spots. He must have been well into his sixties. I wondered if he had thought about returning to our motherland someday to die. But why should he want that? We have no choice about where we were born, yet sometimes we can choose where we die. We owe ourselves a chance to grow up, find home elsewhere, and realize ourselves.

NIYA ARRIVED IN BERLIN on Thursday evening and called me after she reached her friend Aylin's place. We agreed to see each other the next day at three thirty. She would meet me at the train station in Wannsee. She said we could do some sightseeing in that area while we talked. I felt a twinge of uneasiness about the meeting, but I was also looking forward to seeing her. Katie and I emailed each other every day but didn't have much to say. She was busy wrapping up the semester to get ready for her stint in China.

When I got off the train at Wannsee the next afternoon, passing the vegetable and fruit stand in the middle of the underground tunnel to reach the exit, I saw Niya standing on the wide terrazzo stairs that led up to the front hall of the station.

She was dressed in a black single-breasted coat, calf-high suede boots, and sunglasses. Her left shoulder leaned against the wall; her hair was a touch mussed. At the sight of me, her face opened up into a smile, showing her tiny eyeteeth; she hurried over and hugged me. Her coat gave off a faint smell of mothballs. I was caught off guard—we'd never been this close before. I said, "You should be hiding behind a magazine."

"Why?" she asked.

"That would make you more like a detective or a private investigator. More professional, you know."

She swatted my shoulder. "Stop making fun of me."

Together we went out of the station. Lake Wannsee was just across the street, patches of the water visible, flickering feebly against the sunset. I suggested we go to the lakeside, and maybe we could have a boat ride. There were a number of ferryboats in the docks and also signs that announced schedules and stops— Griebnitzsee, Glienicker Lanke, Pfaueninsel—although few people were around. One of the boats was named *Moby Dick*. "Come, let's take a ride on it," Niya said and tugged my forearm.

I liked the sight of that tourist boat. It resembled the Melvillean monstrosity, with jagged teeth, silver sides, a streamlined back, an ebony belly, and huge diamond-shaped scales, half of them bright, the other half dark. But a man on the deck, working with an acetylene torch and a welder's glass, told us that the boats were all docked for the winter. So Niya and I strolled along the lakeside instead, pointing out the moored yachts and birds bobbing on the waves. In the distance, we could see athletes sculling and rowing, their cries echoing on the water, its surface vast like an open bay glimmering in the twilight.

We found a bench and sat down. Niya told me, "I've been talking with Haili. I believe that something terrible is going to happen and that you might get hurt, but I don't know exactly what is going on. She's being so vague, but everything she says about you sounds like a threat."

I nodded, my stomach tightening. "What did she say?"

"She said, 'You're not double-crossing me, Niya, are you?' I told her I wanted to be neutral because the situation had become political, and I didn't want to be involved in politics. She started screaming—she accused me of befriending you and betraying her."

"But what did she say about me?" I asked impatiently.

"She said, 'Danlin is a nonentity now. His actions have made him an enemy of China.' I asked her, 'Don't you have any pity for him? For better or for worse, you must have loved him once.' She said, 'I fell out of love. He wants to destroy others but has brought destruction on himself. If you see him, tell him I will forgive him only if he throws himself at my feet and licks my shoes.'"

"So you have some pity for me?" I asked, my mind raging with misgivings and guesses.

"I confess I do." Niya lowered her eyes, then fixed them on me.

"Still, you are a friend of Haili's."

Niya shook her head. "I no longer feel close to her. In the beginning I knew she'd made a mistake in the way she handled her book deal, but I also believed that you were being vindictive toward her. When I defended her, in a way I wanted to help her make amends while preventing her from being attacked by you and others. But then she became spiteful and brought in the Chinese government to crush you." Niya paused. "We all make the wrong decision sometimes. As long as we correct it in good time, it shouldn't be a big deal. But if one persists in doing the wrong thing, at some point a mistake becomes unforgivable. That's why I cannot align myself with Haili anymore. I often wonder what made her change so much. She's become addicted to publicity and fame, and will do anything to chase after attention."

I looked into Niya's eyes. The limpid honesty in them convinced me of the truth of her words. "Do you think Haili will file more lawsuits?" I asked. "Could that be what she's talking about?"

"She said litigation was useless against a pauper. She seems to have given up on trying to attack you legally."

"Then what's going on?"

"She sounded euphoric," Niya said cynically. "Something bad must have happened to you to have brought her that much joy."

"But you don't know anything beyond what she said?" I cried. "Why did you even come here?"

"Don't be angry that I don't have the full story," Niya protested. "And I didn't come just to spoil your trip. I also came to see my friend."

"I'm not mad," I said, trying to keep my voice steady, "just worried. Thanks for letting me know what you've heard."

"There is one other thing," she said slowly. "Larry seems to be involved now."

"How is he involved?"

"Haili said Larry had given her a big loan. She was so happy she nearly burst her seams. But I don't know how much she got from him."

"With money she can do a lot." I gave a little moan as I thought about it. "She can use a hotshot attorney, she can hire hacks to write articles, she can bribe more officials—"

"I guess so." Niya sighed and looked a little plaintive.

"Come on, help me think. What can they do to me?"

"I tried—I've been trying the whole way here. I truly can't fig-

ure out what's going on. Before leaving New York I called Haili
again to see if she could tell me anything else, but she wouldn't
divulge a thing."

The dusk deepened, and a breeze swept by and shook the
sailboats in a nearby dock, many of them covered with tarps
of various colors. Their masts tilted and wavered, the riggings
tinkling fitfully, while gentle waves lapped the concrete blocks
of the bank. A large flock of waterfowl—mallards, white-billed
coots, geese, swans, even a mandarin duck—paddled over.
They seemed hungry, looking at us inquiringly. I wished I had
some bread or popcorn or chips for them. Winter would be
hard for these birds. Where would they find food? I wondered.
Why hadn't they flown south? How were they going to survive
the cold weather? There must be an island close by where they
nested.

"I like swans," Niya said. "The way they always stay in pairs,
male and female. What's that one?" she asked, pointing.

"A mandarin duck," I told her.

"I never saw a mandarin duck before," Niya said thought-
fully. "Don't they always live in pairs too?"

"I don't know," I said honestly. "Maybe only in folklore.
Summer must be nice here."

"It's gorgeous in spring and summer," Niya said, her voice
lifting. "Sailboats, birds, flowers, and kids everywhere. Down
there the beach is open for people to swim in the lake. You
should come again."

"Are you hungry, Niya?" I asked, suddenly feeling restless.

"Famished."

I offered to take her to the restaurant I'd mentioned in my
email, but she wanted to try an Indian restaurant that Aylin
particularly liked. Together we headed west along Königstrasse
toward that place. Niya said she was leaving with Aylin for Dres-

den the next morning. She was captivated by pictures of the castle there, and had been wanting to see it for a long time.

The Indian restaurant was a long walk from the lakeside. I strolled in the reddish path on the sidewalk, along the curb. Finally Niya pulled me out of it, saying that it was for cyclists. I began to see that indeed all bicycles ran in the five-foot-wide strip paved with terrazzo squares. Few Germans that we passed were overweight, and they all followed the traffic rules strictly, waiting for green lights when they crossed streets, even if there was no car in sight.

The restaurant was a fine place, clean and quiet, with a faint smell of incense. The space was well illuminated but not too bright, offering an intimate atmosphere. On each table were a candle and a small vase of striped mums surrounding a tiny sunflower. A slim waiter led us to a corner table and lit the candle. As I was ordering a Heineken, Niya stopped me, saying, "Let's have draft beer. In Germany you ought to drink draft beer."

So we each had a tall glass. The beer was excellent, sharp and fresh with a mellow aftertaste. We ordered fish masala and basil chicken, which came with two small salads and naan. Niya said that portions in German restaurants were big, so we shouldn't order anything more for now.

She was right—the two dishes were enough for us. I liked the way they were served, each in a stainless-steel pot sitting on a metal supporter like a tiny stove that had a votive candle burning under the dish to keep it warm. The naan, puffed up in a shallow wicker basket, was delicious. Our mood was lifting.

"This is so good," Niya raved. "I haven't eaten basmati rice in so long."

"I'm glad you like it," I said. "Tell me, Niya, did your parents starve you when you were little?"

"What a question!" She looked at me in shock. "Are you trying to make fun of me?"

"Not at all. Most women from the northeast are tall and sturdy," I pointed out. "But you're so cute and petite, like a beauty from south of the Yangtze."

"You're messing with me again," she said, relaxing, accepting the barbed compliment. "You know, my parents actually urged me to eat more when I was in my early teens, but I could never finish what they gave me. 'You're eating like a bird and won't grow tall,' they kept warning me. But I was too stubborn to listen, and my cousins always ribbed me, saying I was starving myself because I wanted to look like a ballerina. It wasn't until I was eighteen that I began to enjoy my food. By then it was too late for me to grow any more."

"I'm happy you like this rice. I often cook basmati back home." That was true, though I couldn't make it perfectly al dente like what was served here.

"I don't believe you. We don't have this rice in China."

"I mean in New York."

"Are you kidding me? Katie can tell basmati from Nishiki or jasmine rice?"

"It's not that hard to taste the difference," I said, laughing.

"Lucky woman. Haili told me that the Chinese officials had taken Katie away from you. She said, 'Danlin lost his bride. Serves him right.' Is that true?"

"Not really," I said, though Niya's words stung. "Katie and I never planned to marry—we knew we'd go our separate ways sooner or later. And now, since she'll be leaving for her fellowship, the sooner we say good-bye the better. Drawing things out could just become painful."

"You're a good man, Danlin," Niya said, "but you seem

always to have bad luck with women. In Katie's case, perhaps you tried too hard."

"What do you mean?"

"You wanted to save face after Haili left you, didn't you?"

"That was part of it," I admitted. "There was more to it than that."

"Don't try to conceal your vanity," Niya pressed, teasing.

"Honestly, in the beginning I had other concerns."

"What were they?"

"I thought that life might be easier for me if I lived with an American woman. At least my English would improve. In fact, Katie has learned a lot of Chinese from me, in bed. Don't smile like that. I'm telling you the truth. Men are the same as women in most ways—we all look for mates who will improve our lives."

"So, like for Haili, for you marriage was an opportunity?"

"I didn't think of marriage at all, but I did date Katie with an eye to some practical gains. Now I can see I was wrong. She helped me a lot in the beginning, and her warmth loosened me up, but on the whole I've given more than I got."

"I like your honesty, Danlin—you always talk straight. Like I said, I've avoided Chinese men in general, because so many of them feel superior to others, especially to people from provincial places who do menial work."

"So I'm not a typical Chinese man?" I smiled.

"At some level you're not. We're two of a kind." She pointed at herself. "I'm a good woman but have no luck with men. I always meet cheaters, spongers, and sleazebags, so I've realized that I need to be prepared to remain single for the rest of my life."

"You're sure you're a good woman?" I couldn't help asking.

She considered the question seriously. "Well, I'm honest and kindhearted, and I'm capable in the kitchen, in the bedroom, and in the living room."

"The last one I don't get—why in the living room?"

She tittered, wiping her lips with a pink napkin. She said, "I'm good at giving parties. No, I shouldn't say that. I don't like parties that much, but I know how to make guests comfortable—how to be a good hostess." She let out a faint sigh. "If only I could fall head over heels in love again. I'd give an arm for having that feeling back, even just for a week."

I was tempted to say that we'd both outgrown that hormone-crazed phase. But instead I asked her, "What if you could start life over? Would you want to have the same life you've been living?"

"No way!" She shook her head ruefully. "I would've married the boy who first fell in love with me when we were teenagers, but I was so stupid I turned him down out of hand."

"If you go that route," I cautioned, "you might be stuck in a provincial town forever."

"I wouldn't mind," Niya said firmly. "How about you? What would you change?"

"I would want to be born outside of China and to have never set eyes on Yan Haili."

Niya's eyes widened. "She really traumatized you!"

"So did Old China."

The waiter returned to our table and asked how we were enjoying the meal. We answered with praises. His name was Vivek, and he was from Jaipur. He had come to our table time and again, because he said he didn't often get to speak English. He was handsome, slightly frail, and in his mid-twenties, already a father of two. I asked him how often he went back to India. "I go home for a month every winter," he said. "It's cold here."

Unlike Vivek, the other South Asian men working here were

all quite burly, and some joked and passed along their orders in booming voices. One had a shaved head and looked rather fierce.

I left two euros for a tip, wondering as I did so if it was too little. "Eleven percent is more than enough," Niya assured me. "Tips are included in the checks here. People just leave a bit of cash as a token."

Once we stepped out of the restaurant, she added, "Aylin said this place was ruined by Americans being too openhanded."

"You mean Americans tip too much? Then I suppose I am American in that sense. Why not be happy to see others happy?"

"You're a good-hearted man." She clutched my upper arm with both hands and leaned in, pressing her chin against my shoulder.

I wrapped my arm around her to shield her from the chilly wind. We walked like this all the way to her friend's place.

To my amazement, despite her Turkish name, Aylin looked more like an archetype of the fair German woman, with blue eyes and flaxen hair. Her figure was elegant, like that of a model, in her aubergine-colored dress and taupe stockings. She wore opal earrings and silver bracelets. We sat in her perfume-drenched living room and chatted over Rize tea, brewed in a porcelain pot. Aylin said airily that she missed New York, but Berlin was her hometown and she was surrounded by friends and family here—she had gone to the States only to do graduate work. Besides, she had a good managerial job at a hospital now. She spoke English with a soft, melodic accent and lapsed into a German word or phrase from time to time. She talked about her father, who had just returned to his own home city of Istanbul. When she was growing up, the man had kept telling his children that when they were no longer his responsibility, he'd go back to his homeland, but none of them had believed him. When Aylin's youngest brother had graduated from college the year before, their father uprooted himself and made good on his word, despite the family's objections. Aylin's mother had no choice but to follow him.

"Is he happy to be back in Turkey?" I asked.

"He seems to be. He always felt like a foreigner here."

"How long did he live in this country?"

"Twenty-seven years."

I nodded. It was a long time to be away from home. "But how could he readapt after living away from Turkey for so long?"

"The first few months were difficult," Aylin confirmed, "but he and my mother both feel at home now."

"To some extent they're lucky," Niya put in. "They have a homeland they can return to."

"Now my siblings and I will have to go back to visit them at least once a year," Aylin said.

Around nine o'clock I took my leave because the two of them would need to get up early in the morning for the train. Niya came out with me, wrapped her arms around me, and kissed my cheek. "Think of me sometimes, okay?" she asked, her eyes shimmering in the dark.

"I will," I said. "Have a wonderful trip." I turned and headed to the train station, beyond which the moon dangled, a great shining crescent.

The nippy air felt a little damp because of the lake nearby. I whistled a little as I walked—I noticed that I'd been in a better frame of mind since leaving New York. I felt calm and enjoyed meeting people. I didn't drop the unsettling remarks that seemed to have become my trademark. Was Berlin so different from New York? I reflected. Probably not. It must have been due to the absence of those three crooks I'd been fending off day and night. My fight with them must have been affecting me within. The constant struggle had been leaching into my heart, threatening to warp my personality. I wished I could spend more time away from the crush of New York. There had to be better ways to live a life.

TWENTY-ONE

I returned to New York fraught with anxiety. When I went in to work the next morning, slightly groggy from the six-hour time difference, I found GNA nearly empty—even the cork bulletin board in the hallway was bare. A thin fluorescent tube flickered above it. Only the door of Wenna's office was open; I could hear her clacking on her keyboard. Puzzled, I went into the break room and found a pot of coffee waiting, just like every morning. I poured myself a cup, about to head to my office, when Kaiming stepped in. He said, "Danlin, can I have a word with you?"

I downed a mouthful of coffee, then followed him to his office. My stomach was tightening—had there been layoffs? The instant I sat down in the chair before his desk, he said, "Our company has changed hands. We all have to go."

"What?" My heart was in my throat. "What do you mean?"

"Jiao Fanping has bought GNA," Kaiming said clearly. "He's the owner now."

I stared at Kaiming, at a loss for words. He repeated, "Jiao has bought our company."

"But how could *you* let this happen? You invested so much of your life in GNA—we were the only independent Chinese-language news agency left in the West."

"Don't forget I'm also a businessman." He frowned and sucked his teeth as if to soothe a toothache.

"What happened to your dream of becoming a modern-day

Joseph Pulitzer? Don't you want to be remembered as a pioneer figure in the history of Chinese journalism?" As I was speaking, bile rose in my throat and I swallowed.

He puffed out a sigh, his cheeks swelled and his eyes dim. "What could I do?" he said lamely. "I owned only forty percent of the company's shares. Jiao managed to buy the rest of the shares from the other holders. As a result, he owned more than I did of this company, and I could do nothing but sell him my shares. I'm sorry about the turnover, Danlin, but this is the reality we have to accept."

"Damn it, didn't you already accept the deal before you dispatched me to Germany? Why did you keep me in the dark? I was such a moron to trust you!" I knew Jiao couldn't have made the buyout without the cooperation of Kaiming and some other shareholders. My boss could have easily taken countermeasures to prevent Jiao from acquiring so many shares. Kaiming must have gotten greedy and sold everything for cash. Perhaps all the trouble I'd been making for the Chinese government had helped enhance GNA's value in its eyes. It was a chilling thought, which I had no way to prove.

Kaiming went on, "There was no way we could overcome all the odds against us. The turnover was finalized and will appear in the news today. To some extent, I also came out a loser."

"So we're all fired? Why? Won't they still need staff?"

"Everyone's being replaced by new hires from Beijing. Except for Lucheng," Kaiming said. "He'll stay. Jiao offered me the position of vice director, but I declined. I want to spend a year traveling and reading, to recharge myself and figure out what to do."

"But who are these new reporters?" I sputtered. "Government lackeys?"

"You know the editor Gu Bing?"

"What about him?"

"He was supposed to head the new team, but he changed his mind because he has an important project at hand, editing a large volume of the Party's history as a gift for the sixtieth anniversary of the People's Republic, so someone else will come and run the editorial office."

"I guess this is it." I took a mouthful of the brackish coffee and believed I finally understood what Niya had told me about Larry's loan to Haili.

"I'm sorry about the situation you are in." Kaiming slid open his drawer, took out his checkbook, and ripped out a check already written. "Here's a token of my thanks for the yeoman work you did for more than three years. I hope this can help tide you over till you find a job."

I thanked him and took the check for two thousand dollars, his personal gift to me. Clearly, nobody had been given severance pay. The check felt light in my pocket as I walked back to my office.

Before I collected my things, I talked with Wenna and found out more about the takeover. The agency had been sold for more than $16 million, and Kaiming was offered $6.5 million. It was impossible for him to resist such a deal. But how could Jiao Fanping have so much capital? Did he get it from Haili?

"Not from her," Wenna answered, waving her hand and blinking her eyes. "Your ex owns only a small percentage of the company. She and her husband invested one million dollars in GNA. Jiao is the real owner."

"Is he that rich?" I couldn't imagine him getting that kind of money.

"Well, he got a huge loan from the Chinese government." Wenna gave a wry smile. "Have you heard of China's campaign for acquiring the right of speech?"

I snorted. "Yes, I have." I mimicked a senior official who had recently declared: "'Only when we have the right of speech can the world really accept our country as a global player. Comrades and friends, let us rally all the forces to fight the West's demonization of China.'"

Wenna laughed, rubbing her pudgy nose with the knuckle of her forefinger. "The Chinese government has been spending billions of dollars acquiring and establishing media facilities abroad so its voice can influence the world's opinions in the same way as the mainstream Western media."

"I know they're eager to set up their own type of CNN and BBC," I said, nodding. "But GNA was just a tiny business."

"Well, that depends on how Jiao and the powers behind him presented GNA to the government. I heard that even some small, sleazy newspapers in Taiwan and Hong Kong were sold to the mainland for millions of dollars apiece. The Chinese government is flush with cash and has been acquiring all kinds of junk. But I've also heard there's some talk in Beijing about how to purchase *The New York Times*."

The idea was absurd—but then, so was everything that had already happened. "Still," I persisted, "how will Jiao ever pay back the loan? He can't possibly make a lot of profit from this news business."

"That doesn't bother him. It's not his own money he's burning anyway. The government might write off the loan as a loss eventually, like its other failed projects."

I shook my head, brooding over everything I'd just learned. "Do you think the Chinese government will ever dominate the media the way they want to?"

"Hard to tell." She smiled, her just-whitened teeth gleaming a little. "In any event, for me it's time to quit."

I realized that this was a great opportunity for all the former shareholders of the company to take profits. There had been seven or eight of them—some employees who had been given shares as part of their compensation, some outside investors. They had become millionaires overnight. Wenna must be one of them.

"What are you going to do?" I asked, viewing her with new envy.

"I'll go back to Tianjin in January."

"Really? You're giving up journalism?"

"Is there genuine journalism in China?" she asked drily. "Why should I bother with it? I owned seven percent of GNA. I sold Jiao my shares, so it's time for me to start another life."

Despite my amazement, I said, "Best of luck."

"Thanks very much," she said cheerfully. "Maybe I'll open a bookstore near a college campus in Tianjin."

"You could set up a chain like Barnes and Noble."

"No, I need just one store with a little café in it so that customers can sit down and read books if they cannot afford to buy them."

"Whatever you do," I said, "you'll become a successful businesswoman."

She ignored my attempt at irony and said, "Danlin, I'm sorry you lost your job. But you're a smart man and I know you'll make it one of these days."

"Goodness knows, that day could be light-years away. Does Kaiming still own the publishing house?"

"Only a quarter of it. Jiao is the real owner."

That dashed my hope of continuing to work for Kaiming. I couldn't believe how quickly he had abandoned his dream of publishing his own newspaper and magazine around the world. I realized I might be the only loser in the takeover. I felt like Don Quixote, the Knight of the Sorrowful Face, charging at windmills with a broken lance and only getting himself dismounted and battered.

"Oh my, look at this!" Wenna turned her monitor to me. On the screen was a page of Tencent news that showed a photo of Haili holding aloft with one hand the first page of a contract while she beamed, the outer corners of her eyes tilting up. Her other hand held a brand-new copy of her novel, the Chinese original. Larry stood behind her, smiling with one hand in his jacket pocket and his other hand giving a thumbs-up. Above them was the headline FAMOUS AUTHOR SELLS HER MOVIE SCRIPT TO HOLLYWOOD.

I skimmed the article, fighting a pointless sense of panic. The piece outlined the transaction as a joint venture between the Great Wall Movie Studio and Shocket Pictures, a company based in L.A. The price of the script was more than a million dollars, according to the report, which characterized the deal as great progress in the two countries' cultural exchange. More Chinese actors would soon be bound for Hollywood to act in the film. Haili told the reporter, "Now, everyone can see who's a liar. Feng Danlin should find a crack on the ground and hide in there like an earthworm that can make no noise."

"Do you believe this is real?" I asked Wenna.

"Whether I believe it or not is irrelevant," Wenna said cryptically. "She has a contract in hand now and must be in seventh heaven."

"But this is so different from what she claimed," I said, getting angry once more. "She didn't sign with Panorama Pictures. The film will certainly be bankrolled by the Chinese side."

"I know that, and you know that," Wenna said, a little sadly, "but we both also know that the public never cares about those kinds of details."

"I guess they might no longer care whether Haili's novel will appear in other languages either."

"I think that the movie will overtake everything," Wenna said, scanning the article once more. "From now on, they'll start talking about which star should join the cast, how big the budget is, where it should be shot, et cetera, et cetera."

Her words made me realize that there would be no point writing about Haili's fraudulence anymore. According to the article, Haili was going to be the manager of the Dolphin Publishing House, a new company, based in Brooklyn and owned by Jiao Fanping, that would bring out fine art books, translated classics, nonfiction, and posters. She had triumphed with the support of the Chinese state. How lucky it is to have a big country behind you! If only you didn't have to obey it like a mutt, with drooping ears and downcast eyes, or have to learn when to wag your tail and when to tuck it between your legs.

With heavy steps and a stuffed backpack slung over my shoulder, I lugged myself out of GNA. The northwesterly wind whistled, biting at my back. My bike creaked as I pedaled along—since I would likely never be coming back here, I'd have to take it on the train back to Flushing. It was overcast, the sky slate gray, and dead leaves skittering across the road. I felt myself floundering, as if my very world was crumbling.

TWENTY-TWO

"What do you plan to do?" Niya asked me, her chin propped on one hand. We were sitting in Lovely Songs in downtown Flushing.

"I'm not sure," I said, squeezing a slice of lime into my tequila. "Maybe I can work as a carpenter—my father taught me the trade when I was growing up. I know this guy, Randy, at a construction company. He said he might take me on when I needed a job."

A giggle burst out of Niya's lips; then a bubbling sound sizzled in her nose as if she was suppressing a laugh. I asked, offended, "What's so funny? Is that such a bad idea? Carpenters can make good money."

"No, no, I admire that. Whether you rise or fall, you can always survive, Danlin. You're a man." She lifted her ginger ale and took a large sip, then continued. "I saw Haili yesterday, and she wanted me to pass a message to you."

"What did she say?"

"She'd like to offer you a job at the Dolphin Publishing House." Niya widened her eyes. "See, like I said, she can be very generous."

"What kind of job?" I asked, certain that the offer wasn't as generous as Niya believed.

"Maybe an accountant."

"More likely a bookkeeper, because I don't have a certificate in accounting. She knows I'm too honest to embezzle funds."

"You should appreciate her kind gesture, shouldn't you?" Niya said warmly. "I think she might still have feelings for you."

For a moment I considered her words. Then I realized that Haili couldn't have initiated the job offer—it must be a trap laid by the trio. I shook my head and said, "Tell her I can always work as a carpenter. I can do without them—I'm above them."

"Why can't you be more conciliatory?" Niya prodded. "She meant to help you."

"She couldn't have made such an offer on her own," I snapped, unable to hide my annoyance. "They want to control me. Once my livelihood is in their hands, I won't be able to write anything against them. And Haili knew I might not accept an offer from her directly, so she had you be the messenger. Of course, it's all supposed to demonstrate how magnanimous she is."

"I see," said Niya, looking sheepish. "Then you should avoid them."

I took another sip of my drink to calm down. But I couldn't quell my curiosity for long. "What has Haili been doing these days?"

"She and Larry are planning to go to China to adopt a child."

"A baby?" I rubbed my eyebrows.

"Yes, a girl, two years old. I saw a photo of her. She's lovely."

"I never knew Haili liked children." In the years we were together, she'd never once mentioned a desire to become a parent.

"She said she was dying to become a mother." Niya shrugged. "Every woman feels that way at some point in her life."

"So Larry and she can't have a baby of their own?"

"It seems not."

"Well," I conceded, "I have to admit they're doing something good if they can give the child a stable home. There are far too many abandoned baby girls in China."

"They've also been hunting for an apartment. They want to buy a place in Chelsea."

"Pricey!" I noted. "So the movie deal is real?"

"Absolutely, it's a joint venture—the Chinese side has agreed to provide seventy-five percent of the budget."

"She'll get her million dollars?"

"I believe so."

"See," I said, driving my point home bitterly, "it always pays to serve a big country, even if you sell your soul in the process."

"Well." Niya blinked. "Is your soul too expensive for sale?"

"Without a doubt," I said wearily. "It's priceless."

"No wonder Haili calls you a megalomaniac." Niya laughed. "But I like you for that."

I laughed too, put my hand over hers, and gave it a shake in gratitude. Her fingers felt dry but warm. "Who knows?" I said. "Maybe I'm just too proud, and too stupid to give in."

"I don't think you should do carpentry, though," Niya said seriously. "You have more meaningful things to offer."

"Like my articles?" I snorted. "No one seems to want those anymore."

"We both know you have readers all over the world," said Niya, ignoring my scorn. "You were already voted a public intellectual by those readers, and you should fulfill that role, shouldn't you? Didn't you say you'd like to live up to that title?"

"But I don't have a platform anymore. Where would I publish? How will people hear me? Even if I were to start a blog on my own, I'd still need a paying job so I can survive." I took a gulp of my tequila. "And another thing—I don't think writing articles is more meaningful than making furniture. It's just something I'm good at."

"In any case, if I were you, I'd go to grad school and do a PhD," Niya said, undaunted.

"That would take years, and that's if I'm lucky enough to get into a graduate program in the first place."

Niya let out her breath in frustration. "You Chinese men—you only think of speed, always looking for a way as effortless as eating noodles. I believe there's only one way to do one thing right—and that's usually the hardest way. Now, you're not a real intellectual yet, but it's not too late for you to grow into one. If I were you, the last thing I'd do is resign myself to chance."

"It's always easier said than done," I said stubbornly.

"Think about it, okay?"

That softened me some. "You believe that going to grad school is the only way for me to become a real intellectual?"

"Is there an alternative?"

I nodded, seeing her point. "I'll think about it."

When Niya got up go to the ladies' room, I saw that she'd left a copy of the magazine *Open* on top of her coat on the extra chair. The cover featured the Ping-Pong player Lili Liu, who had just won the Asian championship, representing Japan. I knew her story and began leafing through the article. Originally she'd been trained on China's national team and often participated in international competitions. Once, at a top world game, the coaches of the Chinese team ordered her to let a teammate win the final match so that China could secure more medals, and she agreed. But when she and the teammate got into the final round, Liu played furiously and routed her opponent three to zero. Although Liu won the gold and China didn't lose any of the expected medals, she was dismissed from the national team and banned from all domestic and international games, including the Olympics. Then, to everyone's surprise, she married a Japanese man, left China, and resumed training in Tokyo. Six years later, once naturalized, she reemerged, representing her adopted country at the Asian Games. The

Chinese national team ignored her, considering her nothing more than a has-been, but Lili Liu, wreaking vengeance, played vehemently and, one after another, defeated all the top Chinese players. Whenever she scored a point, she would shout, in Japanese, "Gotcha!" When Chinese reporters interviewed her after her victory, she spoke only Japanese. Her defiance infuriated millions of Chinese Ping-Pong fans, who condemned her as a traitor, and some threatened to trash her parents' home in Shanghai.

"Well, what do you make of her? Isn't she something?" Niya asked about Lili Liu when she'd sat down again.

"I can't blame her for what she did," I said, putting the magazine on the chair. "The country betrayed her first—she was justified."

"I disagree. She went too far and spat at China."

"But the country had wrecked the six or seven best years of her career, and it's understandable that she would be angry. I take her defiance as a way of asserting her existence."

Niya shook her head, unconvinced. "The coaches of the national Ping-Pong team don't stand for the country, just as the Communist Party doesn't represent China."

"Who represents China then?" I demanded. "You or I, or the waitress over there, or the bartender behind the counter? Or those two dissidents in Maryland who just apologized to the Dalai Lama on behalf of all the Chinese? At this point in history, the Communist Party is in fact the country because it rules China and sits on the UN Security Council. It's naïve to maintain the distinction between the state and the ruling party, because every high official in China is a Party member—the Party has made itself identical with the country. The truth is that a country is not a god, it's a historical construct. It's foolish to imagine the country as a mystical figure, a generous mother that has raised all the Chinese, who in return must be obedient, longing for her love and nurturance. That's a fallacy, a lie."

"Wait a second," Niya broke in. "I object! I believe we must maintain the distinction between the country and the ruling power, just as I love China but hate the Chinese government. Shame on you for what you just said."

"Well, let me tell you a story. The other day I read in *The Sing Tao Daily* that five men in Taiyuan City had burned themselves because their homes had been torn down by a demolition crew so a hotel could be built on the same site. Because the country owned the land, to which those families had only users' rights, they had to surrender their homes. Once their homes were gone, life no longer had any meaning for them. The five men believed that their deaths would secure some government funding for their families, so they set themselves on fire. Two of them didn't die, but instead of getting compensation, they were sent to jail in spite of their severe burns. At first they were charged with arson—then that was changed to 'incitement to public discontent.' Now, do you think those men would maintain the same distinction you do—it was the local officials, not the country, that destroyed their homes? The country is always good and only the corrupt local officials are bad—would they think that way? The officials didn't make the law, nor do they own the land. They work for the government, but what does the government represent? The country." I paused, then said, more quietly, "I've been thinking about those men ever since I read their story. It's been gnawing at me. I'm sure they felt that it was the country, the owner of all China's land, that made their livelihood impossible. The fact is that whoever holds state power speaks of the country. I simply don't buy the nonsense that the country is a benign, magnanimous matriarch that spawned and raised all the citizens, who in turn must behave like filial children bowing down to her will. That's a lullaby, a fetish for dopes, or a tall tale that corrals people into servitude. I have outgrown all that. If a country misbehaves, people have every right to rein it in, give it a good kick in the ass, and fix it. This is the responsibility of the citizens."

"What a fine load of bull you just let out. That's sacrilege." Niya scowled at me, her eyes ablaze. "You must maintain some difference between the country and the state."

"No, I won't," I insisted. "The powers that be never use the word *state* when they brainwash people and condemn dissidents. They've always kept themselves as identical as possible with the country so that they can appear legitimate and sacred. Anyone against the totalitarian government is classified and punished as a traitor to the country. It's time for us to look the country in the face and debunk its myth and sanctity."

"Then you'll only make a fool of yourself."

"You think the idea of the country is sacred, then?" I demanded.

"Not the idea," Niya admitted, "but China, the actual land, is holy to me. It has a pull on me that I can't explain."

I was speechless for a moment. Then I said calmly, "I can weigh a country only on how it serves the common person. I reserve my right to have contempt for any country. For me, a country is no more than a dog, a people's guard dog, so it would be unreasonable for a dog to demand that its owners love and worship it. It ought to be grateful that people care for it and don't let it starve."

"You're outrageous!" Niya sputtered.

A silence followed. I was about to remind her that her father had once said China was a country that devoured its people and that he'd urged her to flee, but I refrained. With my finger I wiped away the remaining salt from the rim of my glass and took a swig of the tequila. I realized that she had projected too much religious feeling onto our native land—the longer and the farther she lived away, the more attachment and love she developed toward it. She would have done better to join a church or temple.

"Anyway," Niya said finally, without looking at me, "think about grad school."

I half-joked, "Tell me, if I go to some remote town to do graduate work, will you come with me?"

"Out of the question," she responded promptly. "Unless you come to your senses and change your attitude toward our motherland."

"That may not happen." I went on, joking, "I've been trying to become a Buddhist who achieves enlightenment and deliverance by abandoning his origins. I can develop no attachment to any place."

"You'll never become a Buddhist," Niya scoffed. "You're full of material desires, and your sense of self is too strong."

"I can see China lying between us like a third party. In fact, even if I succeed in getting you into bed, I can't get hard with a cold country stretching out between us. For the life of me I can't handle that—it's so difficult to fuck a country, impossible unless you're its president or premier."

She stared at me in astonishment, then broke into laughter. "You have a perverse imagination. You're crazier than me."

I too laughed, nervously. I added, "I can't comprehend why a country can fuck a citizen whenever it feels the need, while the citizen can never fuck it back. Why? This question really boggles the mind."

"You've got one hell of a mouth. Don't ever talk like that in front of others or you'll get into big trouble."

I shrugged, undaunted. "I'm already in big trouble."

We parted, still friends, though a hot lump in my throat made me light-headed and caused me to breathe hard. Stepping out of the bar and heading in a different direction than Niya, I tried to buoy myself up by humming an old movie theme song, "Not Afraid to Go Solo":

Sweetheart, do you still dream of the wild?
How often I asked you when we could go away,
Go far, far away.
You always shook your head and smiled,
Saying till I had a truck to my name . . .

I wasn't particularly fond of the tune, yet it churned in me and poured out of my mouth. In my mind's eye I saw the heartbroken young man loading his pickup, about to start out for the wilderness and leave his girlfriend for good. Ahead of me, the street was almost deserted, only a flock of grackles roosted in a leafless treetop, as motionless as if they were napping. A crosswind blew up and set a Styrofoam take-out container tumbling away. It flew past an overturned shopping cart on the curb. I crooned the song over and over on my walk home, though I garbled some lines and was never quite in tune.

I couldn't see the point in doing graduate studies. For now I needed a job so I could pay the bills. Kaiming's two thousand dollars wouldn't last long.

That evening I mentioned grad school to Katie, who surprised me by saying it wasn't a bad idea. In America, she assured me, most PhD students in the humanities and social sciences received financial aid—they were paid to specialize in the impractical fields. The scholarships could be meager but were enough to live on. That's why there were so many perpetual grad students. "I can write an excellent recommendation for you," Katie told me. "But you must make me happy tonight."

"I'll try," I said.

The next day I ran into Lucheng in front of Citibank, and I talked with him about the prospect of graduate studies. He had always been resourceful and wise in a worldly way; for that I respected him. To my surprise, he urged me to apply to grad school, saying he wished he could have done that when he arrived in the States eleven years before. He mentioned some dissidents in North America and said they all had been offered admission to graduate school in the early days of their exile, but they forfeited the opportunities, believing it would be more comfortable and glamorous to be political activists and public figures. They even foolishly thought China would reopen its door to them soon, so there was no need to study hard here. "Look how they're doing now," Lucheng said and snubbed out his cigarette in the dirt in a flowerpot. "They've all become spongers of a sort and depend on the charity of political organizations. You mustn't live like that. Don't ever become a hanger-on. Try to be self-sufficient."

Lucheng's words impressed me deeply, but I still couldn't make up my mind.

FOR DAYS I BROODED about what to do. The thought of going to grad school saddened me, because I was already thirty-six and would have to take the GRE, for which I'd need two or three months to prepare. In addition, I would have to spend hundreds of dollars on application fees. Then I came across an article about a recent controversy over Calvin Elliot, a professor at a state university in California. The man had spoken publicly against the Iraq War, condemning it as an imperial invasion of the Mideast, and declared that it was waged only for control of oil resources, that the United States had never supported human rights in the Arab world, and that the export of democracy in this case was a hoax, a travesty. Despite torrents of condemnations against him, despite several congressmen urging that he be fired from his job, his university refused to let him go, defending its decision on the grounds of preserving academic freedom. I was greatly impressed and moved by the school's position. It made me realize that it was not coincidental that public intellectuals like Noam Chomsky and Edward Said held professorships at universities, which must be the last sanctuaries for freedom of speech. So I decided that I would apply.

Katie helped me gather a list of schools. For my applications I needed three recommendations. Katie agreed to write one, and I thought about asking Rudolph, but she said that might be inappropriate because he had never taught me and was unfamiliar with my work. Not knowing another academic, I turned to Niya and Kaiming; both of them were glad to write on my behalf. My former boss wrote his letter in Chinese and asked Wenna to translate it. For days I worked on my personal statement. I wrote that I wished to study the role the state played in the English and the Chinese media—how governments used the media for propaganda and educational purposes, to provoke or divert public anger and foster patriotism, and how the media contributed to preserving and distorting collective memories. (Katie said there was considerable scholarship already on the English media, and my project would be more viable if I made it a comparative study.) In my applications I was candid about my poor qualifications, since I hadn't been a political science major and would have to start from scratch in some coursework. More problematic, without GRE scores, I'd have to apply with incomplete forms, but I couldn't bear to wait. Not having any published writing samples in English, I attached my unpublished article on the scandal of Haili's novel as proof that I could write in this language. Every one of my applications felt like a long shot.

TWENTY-THREE

Katie left for China two weeks ago. We were in email contact; she seemed to be settling down at Henan University and was pleased about the arrangements with the sociology department there. She was excited about her field research, ready to head for the countryside to interview AIDS victims, many of whom had been blood sellers and had contracted the virus from contaminated needles. I urged her not to rush, given that she had plenty of time. She mustn't eat at street food stands too often, not because the foods might be unclean but because it would take months for her to get used to them. Also, she had to be careful not to endanger herself and those who helped her. Even if the police didn't shadow her, they might harass her helpers.

As I had predicted, soon she began to complain about the obstacles she encountered. It was clear that the authorities would do anything to frustrate her. She wasn't sure she could get access to the AIDS victims at all and was beginning to feel she had been deceived about the fellowship. All the same, she didn't say anything about returning to New York anytime soon—I gathered that if she couldn't conduct the interviews in the countryside, she might go to Beijing and spend the spring semester as a research fellow at China's Academy of Social Sciences. It would be a rare opportunity nonetheless. Besides, there was plenty of her beloved nightlife there.

Her messages often discomfited me, and I could tell that she was becoming obsessed with her scholarship and career. But I didn't complain, not wanting to put more pressure on her. Before long, men were sure to hit on her, an attractive young woman full of brains and energy. Probably not a small number of people there considered her a knockout, her beauty amplified by the fact that she was American.

Soon after the New Year, I got a phone call from a Professor Gambrell at the State University of New York at Buffalo. He explained gently, "According to our guidelines, we cannot admit you into our program if you haven't taken the GRE. I am calling to let you know we are very impressed with you as a candidate, but we haven't received your scores yet. Can you have them sent right away?"

I said, "To be honest, I haven't taken the test yet. I would have to spend at least a couple of months brushing up."

"I am sorry to hear that. Without the GRE, even if we accepted you, you wouldn't get approved by the graduate school that has the final say. But we hope you will apply again next year."

"I will do that," I said.

He went on, "We were very moved by your application, particularly by one of your recommenders, a Chinese woman. She confirmed the story you mentioned in your statement: your news agency had just been purchased by China and you had lost your job. You could do carpentry and make a decent living by working for a construction company, but you want to become a public intellectual, because you still have a sizable readership in Chinese and you aspire to remain an honest voice. That said, rules are rules—we cannot admit you without a complete application."

"I understand," I said, rather let down.

After the phone call, I stood at my window for a long time,

amazed that they had taken Niya's recommendation seriously, even though she was not an academic. To my mind, she was a patriotic hothead, but why hadn't I just ignored her? Why had I kept her as a friend and even cherished our friendship? Was this because subconsciously I wanted to persuade her to agree with me? Or because I was attracted to her passionate love for the country that dominated her? I was not sure. Probably both.

It was snowing, fat flakes floating slantwise, accumulating on the trees, on the arms of the streetlamps, filling the air and muffling the sound of traffic. A scrawny fellow bundled in an overcoat trudged along the sidewalk. It was the homeless man who had a cauliflower ear like a small mushroom and spoke Mandarin with a Shandong accent, and who often sat down at my table when I ate in a dumpling joint or pizzeria. Sometimes I stopped halfway and let him have the rest of the food.

Suddenly he slipped and fell. He picked himself up and stamped the snow vengefully, then waddled away, his dark blue overcoat dappled. In weather like this, he would probably have to spend the night at the shelter at St. George's Church.

Perhaps in essence, my loneliness was no different from his, but this didn't bother me anymore; perhaps because to be alone is a precondition of independence. ("How can you feel lonesome? There're more than six billion people out there," Niya once reproached me.) I thought of calling Niya in the evening to tell her that I'd heard from a university. Professor Gambrell's call had given me a glimmer of hope, though I couldn't yet envision myself as a scholar. My future was unclear, but I knew I would continue to speak out. Whenever a boat emerged loaded with lies and hypocrisy, whatever flag it flew, I would report it to the world.

ACKNOWLEDGMENTS

I would like to thank LuAnn Walther, Catherine Tung, and Lane Zachary for their support, patience, and enthusiasm. At different stages, some friends of mine read the manuscript in progress and gave me invaluable advice. To them I am grateful: Askold Melnyczuk, Ulrike Ostermeyer, Sigrid Nunez, Chitra Divakaruni, and Perry Link.

Ha Jin left his native China in 1985 to attend Brandeis University. He is the author of seven previous novels, four story collections, three volumes of poetry, and a book of essays. He has received the National Book Award, two PEN/Faulkner Awards, the PEN/Hemingway Foundation Award, the Asian American Literary Award, and the Flannery O'Connor Award for Short Fiction. In 2014 he was elected to the American Academy of Arts and Letters. Ha Jin lives in the Boston area and is director of the creative writing program at Boston University.

A NOTE ON THE TYPE

This book was set in Adobe Garamond. Designed for the Adobe Corporation by Robert Slimbach, the fonts are based on types first cut by Claude Garamond (c. 1480–1561). Garamond was a pupil of Geoffroy Tory and is believed to have followed the Venetian models, although he introduced a number of important differences, and it is to him that we owe the letter we now know as "old style." He gave to his letters a certain elegance and feeling of movement that won their creator an immediate reputation and the patronage of Francis I of France.

Typeset by Scribe, Philadelphia, Pennsylvania

Printed and bound by Berryville Graphics, Berryville, Virginia

Designed by Iris Weinstein